CLEAR PATH

A BODHI KING NOVEL NO. 9

MELISSA F. MILLER

PART I

Vipassana: a Pali term that means to see things clearly, as they truly are. Also, insight.

1

GAP Mile 80.4, Union Hill, Pennsylvania

The sun slanted through the dusty window and carved a line across the woman's weathered face. Rory snapped a photo timed to capture both the sunbeam highlighting the dust motes in the air and the contrast of the shadow falling across the woman's left cheek and the peeling wallpaper behind her. She circled the woman on quick, silent feet as she pressed the shutter release button on her Nikon D850, set to quiet continuous release to be as unobtrusive as possible.

Lowering the viewfinder, she asked a question to put her subject at ease. "What year did your parents build this house?"

"Oh, heavens, my parents didn't build it. My grandparents did." Lydia Hudson smoothed the skirt of her dress, the blue material shiny with age.

Rory had told her to dress comfortably, but she was unsurprised when Lydia opened the door wearing her church dress and glossy red lipstick. People couldn't help themselves—it was one of many reasons she preferred spontaneous shoots. Her best work always seemed to come from approaching a stranger at a bus stop and asking permission to snap a photo or stumbling onto an eye-catching natural composition.

But the circumstances dictated she make an appointment for this shoot. She reminded herself what was at stake and re-engaged the woman.

"Really? Do you know when that was?" She raised the camera again and waited.

She started snapping again when Lydia screwed up her face and tried to recall.

After a beat, Lydia spoke softly, her voice echoing off the bare walls. The home had already been emptied of furniture, clothing, belongings. Only memories remained now.

"Must have been, oh, a little over a hundred years ago. They lived here for fifty-some years. When they passed, both of them, one after the other in '72, my mom and dad moved us in here. My brothers got married and moved away, but I stayed to help them out. After I met Ed, rest his soul, we rented a place across the road—that yarn shop and the pottery studio used to be duplex apartments." She gestured out the window at the pair of upscale boutiques across the street.

Rory followed the motion and aimed her viewfinder toward the shops. She fired off a handful of quick shots through the streaked windows to capture the contrast between the past and present of Railroad Way.

She turned her attention back to Lydia. "You lived right across the street?"

A ghost of a smile crossed her red lips as she nodded. "I wanted to stay close. Then, after my parents passed, we moved over here with the kids. I guess I always thought one of them would take the place over when I was gone. Never imagined I'd outlive it."

Lydia's lower lip trembled. Rory pressed the shutter button before the woman could steel her expression.

The Hudsons' home was destined to be demolished in just a few hours. After Lydia repeatedly refused to sell to a developer, the town instituted eminent domain proceedings on the grounds that Lydia was the lone holdout standing in the way of economic development. Rory had heard the gossip just that morning, a murmured conversation she'd overheard in the coffee shop while waiting for her latte and muffin. She asked around until she found someone who knew Lydia's phone number, then called and introduced herself.

She'd expected to have to convince Lydia to let her intrude on such a private moment, but Lydia agreed without hesitation. So Rory had canceled her breakfast order, grabbed her camera equipment, and rode her bike down the trail to document Lydia's farewell to her home and its demolition.

The subject matter was a perfect fit for *Push/Pull*, Rory's upcoming exhibition. If she was lucky, she'd have time to add some of today's photos to the exhibit.

Even if not, the day wouldn't be wasted. She wanted the installation to be a living record and planned to expand it online and possibly in her studio after the gallery exhibit was over.

"Are you going to stay and watch?" she asked quietly, not sure what Lydia would say.

She considered what she would do in Lydia's shoes—would she bear witness to the destruction of her family home or would she leave before the demolition team arrived in hopes of keeping her memories intact?

Lydia squared her jaw and straightened her shoulders. She nodded.

"Are any of your kids coming up to be with you?"

She sniffed. "No, they think I'm a foolish old woman. They think I should just have taken the money and moved to a retirement community someplace warm and sunny." Her voice held no bitterness but was tinged with sadness.

"I'll stay, but I won't photograph it." Rory offered on an impulse. It suddenly felt too invasive, too ghoulish, to record the demolition with Lydia watching.

Lydia's eyes snapped up to meet hers. Her gaze was no longer sad nor tired—it was fierce.

"Oh yes, you will. I'm not going to pretend this didn't happen. You take all the photographs you want, young lady—of me and the house." Her voice shook again, but Rory could tell it was rage, not sorrow, causing this quaver.

She nodded. "Understood."

She waited on the bowed front porch while Lydia took one final, private walk through her home. She'd silenced her phone before the session, so now she turned off the do not disturb feature. Before she could return the device to her pocket, it vibrated as it began to deliver a backlog of text and voicemail messages. She glanced down at the screen. She had two missed calls from the Hot Metal Art Gallery, one voicemail message from the gallery's line, and several texts from its owner. She silenced the phone again and slipped it back into her pocket. She'd deal with Tripp later.

2

GAP Mile 148.8, Downtown Pittsburgh

Bodhi King stood and slung his backpack over his shoulder. Then he leaned in through the open door and across the minivan's passenger compartment to pat his friend on the arm. "Thanks for the lift, Saul."

"You got it, buddy. Still don't understand why you can't take normal vacations."

Bodhi smiled.

"I'm serious," Saul persisted. "Whose idea of relaxation involves walking 150 miles?"

"Mine," Bodhi told him.

Saul shook his head. "I'm glad you decided against camping on the trail, at least. That could've been dangerous."

Bodhi gave him a bemused look. "Dangerous? I doubt it. Possibly uncomfortable—to some."

"Right. Who needs comfort?" Saul cracked.

Bodhi would have been happy to rough it, to hang his camping hammock between two trees and be rocked to sleep by the early spring breeze. Instead, he'd decided to stop for meals and shelter in some of the trail towns lining the Great Allegheny Passage. After recent trips to two small towns—one in the mountains of Vermont, one on the Emerald Coast of Florida—he'd become attuned to the unique challenges facing overlooked rural communities and wanted to offer some small measure of support and solidarity as he traveled.

Now, Saul went on. "But I'm serious. It's not safe to sleep on the trail."

Bodhi cocked his head. "What are we talking about here—a twisted ankle? Poison oak? A bear?"

Saul frowned, shaking his head. "I'm just saying ... some portions of the trail may have been taken over."

"Taken over by what?"

"Not what. Whom." Saul's voice dropped. "The city's made a concerted effort to empty the encampment at the trailhead. Apparently, all they accomplished was relocating the homeless further along the trail."

"Not having a home doesn't make a person a threat." He paused. "In fact, if anyone's endangered, it's probably the unhoused people living on the trail."

"How do you figure?"

"They're more isolated and less visible than they were before. And they're further away from accessible social services, shelter, and medical care so they'll be vulnerable to hunger, illness, and the elements."

Saul drew his brows together and screwed up his face in thought. "I never looked at it that way. Still, promise me you'll be careful."

"I always take care, Saul."

"You have a first-aid kit?"

"Of course."

"Do you carry Narcan in it?"

Bodhi blinked. "Well … no."

He'd prepared his first-aid kit in response to any dangers he expected to encounter: bee stings, splinters, wounds, fevers. It hadn't occurred to him that he could come across someone overdosing on opioids.

Saul popped his glove compartment open and gestured inside. "Take a couple."

Bodhi studied the boxes of naloxone nasal spray. "Why do you have these?"

Saul laughed bleakly. "It's a massive problem. The morgues are full of folks who overdosed—especially on fentanyl. These sprays are an easy way to prevent deaths."

Forensic pathologists, unlike most professionals, hated nothing more than a boom in business.

"Sure, but that doesn't explain why *you* have these. Your patients are beyond saving."

"I think everyone should carry naloxone."

"Everyone?"

"Everyone. You know they have it on college campuses now? They train the students how to administer it."

Bodhi paused, considering this. "No, I didn't realize."

"Shopkeepers on the West Coast keep it behind

the counter in case someone collapses on the street in front of their business or in their bathroom. As far as I'm concerned it's basic safety preparedness—like having a defibrillator or a fire extinguisher."

He had a point, Bodhi thought.

"I will take some, thank you." He removed a handful of the spray vials from the compartment and slipped them into the kit in his backpack.

"Hope you don't need to use them. But it's better to have them than not."

They both nodded. Bodhi bobbed his head in a goodbye that Saul returned by mirroring the gesture. Then Bodhi stood and closed the minivan door. Saul gave a small beep as he pulled away.

Bodhi crossed the parking lot, noting the large boulders—hostile architecture—at the trailhead where the encampment had once stood. He took a deep breath and exhaled before his hiking boots landed on the path with a gentle, almost reverent, motion. Then He took his first step on the one-hundred-and-fifty-mile trek from Pittsburgh to Cumberland, Maryland.

After a couple of hours of uneventful walking, he was six miles outside of Pittsburgh when he encountered what Saul had warned of. Three makeshift shelters nestled in a copse of trees just off the trail. The occupants eyed him warily at first, but his calm demeanor and open hands eventually earned him tentative smiles.

Finally, a woman with sunbaked skin and a threadbare coat emerged from the smallest tent, an orange cat perched on her shoulder like a parrot. The cat studied Bodhi with feline indifference, but the woman's gaze held a mix of wariness and pride.

"You have quite a companion," Bodhi observed, his voice soft.

"This is George," she'd replied, stroking the cat's head. "He takes care of the mice, and I take care of him."

George purred in loud agreement.

As she ran her hand over her pet's head and cheeks, the sleeve of her oversized coat slid up and Bodhi noticed the angry red line running along her forearm—clearly infected. Without comment, he kneeled and opened his pack, retrieving his first-aid kit. She allowed him to clean and dress the wound. Aside from one loud gasp, she remained silent during the process.

After he packed up his kit, he offered her a bottle of water and a handful of protein bars, along with enough cash to buy some food for herself and George.

Her eyes conveyed gratitude, and she said simply, "Thanks."

"You're welcome." He gestured toward the other two tents up on the hill. Their occupants hung back in the trees, watching closely. "Do your friends need any medical attention?"

She shook her head.

He removed the rest of his dried foods and snacks from his pack and placed them in front of her along with some more cash. "For your companions."

She turned and waved for them to come down. The other two women shook their heads, still unsure.

"It's okay," he told her. "You can give it to them."

"I'm Gracie," she said suddenly.

He sensed she didn't share her name often or easily. "I'm Bodhi. Have a peaceful day, Gracie. And George."

As he headed back to the trail, Gracie called up to her friends and they began to make their way down the hillside. Bodhi walked on.

3

____

Union Hill

The screen door squeaked open, and Lydia stepped out onto the porch. Her eyes were red and puffy, as was her nose. But her shoulders were squared and her back was straight.

Rory waited in silence while Lydia locked the door. There was no reason to, of course. The home would be a pile of rubble within the hour. But maybe it was a habit, muscle memory. Or, Rory allowed, maybe the woman simply wanted to experience the ritual of securing her home one last time.

Lydia turned away from the door just as the hard-hatted crew arrived in several mud-splattered pickup trucks, followed by a bright yellow excavator that slowly ground to a stop in the front yard. She stepped forward to stand shoulder to shoulder with Rory. She radiated anger like heat.

Rory snapped a photo as a stocky man with close-cropped gray hair emerged from the passenger side of the lead truck. He wore a fleece jacket and clutched a clipboard. The driver hopped out and grabbed a pair of blaze orange safety vests from the truck bed. After shrugging into one, he offered the other to his passenger, who tugged it on over the fleece. Then the pair retrieved hard hats from the footwell of the truck. Behind them, the rest of the crew was doing the same.

"Sam," Lydia muttered the name as if it were a profanity.

Rory lowered her camera and turned toward the older woman. "Pardon?"

She jerked her chin toward the approaching man and flared her nostrils. "Sam Folger. He's the supervisor of the county construction crew. More like destruction crew."

Sam came to a stop in front of the steps to the porch. "Come down from there, Lydia. We're on a schedule."

Rory's eyes widened at his gruff, unsympathetic tone. Lydia seemed unsurprised.

"Go to hell, Sam."

Sam grunted and gave his head a rueful shake. Lydia made a low noise in the back of her throat. It sounded like the warning Rory's childhood cat used to give before she attacked.

The foreman waved Rory and Lydia over. "You ladies need to get out of this area. It's not safe."

Lydia seemed unable to respond, so Rory said, "We'd like to watch."

He frowned. "Not much to see."

In return, Rory gave him a bright smile and waited.

He scratched his neck under the collar of his flannel shirt. "I suppose as long as you cross the street, you'll be safe enough, but you got to keep an eye out for flying debris."

"We will," Rory promised sweetly. "I just need to be close enough to take some photos for Mrs. Hudson."

The man's gaze shifted to Lydia and her stony face. "Why are you doing this to yourself, Lydia?"

Lydia croaked out a laugh. "Funny. Thought you were the one doing this to me, Sam."

His shoulders slumped. "Come on, Lyd. I don't make the decisions. My crew and I are just doing our job."

Lydia's neck muscles twitched and her jaw tightened, and Rory placed a gentle hand on her elbow to lead her across the street before she exploded. They settled atop the low brick wall that fronted the yarn shop. As Rory shifted and folded her long legs lotus-style, Lydia gave her a sidelong look. "You always get what you want?"

Rory shrugged. What was the point of having a face card, if you weren't going to play it? She was beautiful—objectively. It was an accident of genetics. It didn't have anything to do with her; it just *was*. People fell over themselves to please her. It had been that way her entire life, or at least as long as she could remember.

She tried—especially these days—not to misuse it or rely too heavily on it. But she couldn't deny that when she wanted something, almost invariably a bright smile and a sweet voice got the job done. Lydia watched her, waiting for a response.

"You know what they say," she finally answered. "You catch more flies with honey than with vinegar."

Lydia laughed. "Catch those flies while you can. Believe me, one day your looks will fade and you'll be invisible. Happens to us all."

I can't wait, she thought fervently. She meant it with her whole being but refrained from saying it aloud.

Instead, she nodded and pointed toward the house. "They're getting started."

The older woman turned to watch, and they both stood up as the demolition crew confirmed the utilities had been disconnected and set up a row of orange cones. A pair of workers lowered the tailgate of one of the trucks and headed out to the intersection to stop traffic, while Sam consulted the papers on his clipboard. Rory photographed it all, conscious of Lydia standing ramrod-straight beside her.

Then he raised one hand and gestured for the driver to start the excavator. The engine growled to life and the vehicle bumped over the hard earth until the huge bucket attached to the end of its hydraulic arm was lined up with the side of the house. The digger reversed, and its arm rose with a whine until the bucket was high, hovering over the roof of Lydia's home.

It began its slow descent and plowed into the shingles, smashing into the roof and sending a cascade of tar, nails, and wood raining down onto the ground. Lydia inhaled sharply and sank back onto the wall as if her legs could no longer support her. Rory kept snapping pictures.

Over and over, the bucket slammed into the roof until it collapsed. Then the driver moved on to the walls, loudly maneuvering around the house as the bucket swiveled on its track. Dust and debris filled the air. When the excavator stopped, the house was less than a shell.

A worker waved on a gleaming white SUV, which was followed by a roll-off truck carrying a pair of dumpsters. The SUV came to a stop on the road, and the truck swerved around it to park on what had been Lydia's front yard.

The driver's door opened, and a woman emerged from the SUV. She wore oversized sunglasses and a blue tweed designer pantsuit that Rory immediately recognized as a St. John. But not until she pushed the sunglasses up on top of her honey-colored hair did Rory recognize the woman. What was Julie Mason doing here?

"Witch," Lydia spat under breath.

Rory turned to her. "Julie?"

"You know her?"

"She's my landlord. Why would she be here?"

"Because she's the developer who wanted my house. I hope she's happy now. I have half a mind to rip that bottle-blonde hair right out of her head."

Rory blinked and tried to process the news that Julie was behind the eminent domain proceeding. Her brain refused to make sense of it.

Lydia trembled with anger and started to push up from the wall.

"Where are you going?" Rory asked the question

even though she was pretty sure she knew the answer, unfortunately. She didn't relish the thought of pulling the woman off Julie. Of course, Sam would probably break up the fight, right?

Before Lydia could answer or make good on her threat, the bell above the yarn door jangled and the owner stepped outside. The woman stopped mid-stride to gape at the ruins of the house across the road, shaking her head. Then she spotted the women perched on her wall and drew up short. Her hand went to the yellow crocheted scarf at her throat and she twisted the fringe around her fingers. After a moment, she pasted on a brave smile and made her way down the walkway. She stopped at the edge of the wall.

"Lydia ...," she began. Then she faltered.

Lydia turned her attention away from Julie and gave the woman a long, blank look. "Kim," she finally said in a flat voice.

Kim flushed. "I'm so sorry about, well, you know." The scarf fell from her grasp and she twirled her hand toward the demolished structure in a vague gesture.

"Are you, though?"

The woman's flush deepened, and she blinked rapidly behind her glasses. "Of course, I am."

Lydia's gaze flickered over Kim's head and settled on the whimsical front window display at Tangled Skeins. "Seems like you're doing okay. I'm sure having new luxury lofts with a bistro and coffee shop on the first floor will only make business even better for you."

Kim, who apparently had no response to this, scurried to her car.

After a long moment, Lydia turned to Rory. "I've seen enough. I'm leaving."

"Where will you go?" Rory asked.

"My daughter sent me a bus ticket. I'll stay with her while I figure it out."

"I'll call you when I have prints."

Lydia nodded and seemed to deflate—all the fight leaked out of her and her entire body softened and sagged.

Rory watched her walk away. Then she packed up her camera equipment and unlocked her bike from the rack beside the pottery studio. Before she mounted it, her eyes flitted once again toward Julie, who was gesturing toward the house and giving Sam animated instructions about the disposal of the rubble. As if Julie felt the weight of Rory's gaze, she turned and peered toward Rory, raising a hand to shield her face from the sun.

Rory threw her leg over the bicycle and pedaled off before Julie could cross the road and engage her.

4

Julie Mason blocked out the rumble of engines and screech of metal and brick as the bucket truck gathered debris. She had a long checklist to run through with the crew supervisor, and unwavering focus would make this go faster. The sooner she finished, the sooner she could get away from the noise, dust, and chaos of the demolition site.

Some developers reveled in slapping on a hard hat, rolling up their sleeves, and showing up at their active sites. She was not one. Julie didn't enjoy developing projects, she enjoyed having developed projects. It wasn't the act of creation that sparked her passion, but the result. She could be overcome by a wave of joy when sitting at a table at the bistro, the coffee shop, or the wine bar or while taking an exercise class or a pottery class and knowing *she* made this place possible. When she strode through the lobby of one of her apartment buildings or office buildings, a shiver of pride ran through her body.

This part—the dirt, the cacophony, and the

endless details—was the price she paid for that feeling. So she gritted her teeth and muscled her way through it. She turned her attention back to Sam.

He took a breath and launched into what promised to be a long-winded story about a delay in getting one of the permits. She held up a hand, and he stopped droning.

"When do we *need* the permit? The absolute drop-dead date?"

Sam frowned. "Tomorrow. Day after tomorrow at the latest. We need to be able to close the bridge for a few hours to bring in the cement mixer after we get the foundation dug."

"You'll have the foundation ready to pour that soon?" That seemed awfully quick to her.

He scratched his neck and shifted his gaze away from her face to a point over her shoulder. "They don't want to commit the mixer to the project unless we already have the permit. Seems back-assward to me, but ..."

She got it. Sam wouldn't say it aloud, but the equipment company scheduler and the clerk in the permit office had an arrangement. They both wanted her to grease their palms to keep the project moving. There was a time when she'd have railed against the corruption, gone to the county council to complain, dug in her heels and refused to pay a bribe. But Julie hadn't clawed her way through the old-boys' network to become the most successful developer along the GAP by playing by the rules.

"Make it happen. Use the slush fund."

He nodded and they moved on to the next item on her list. Before she could ask about overtime hours, she felt a light tap on her left shoulder. Now what? She suppressed a sigh and turned.

Kim Rush blinked at her and twisted an obviously handmade yellow scarf around her neck in a nervous gesture. Julie tamped down her irritation at the interruption. Kim owned Tangled Skeins. That made her a tenant.

Julie smoothed her expression into one of friendly concern. "Is something the matter, Kim? I hope the noise and mess won't impact your foot traffic too much, but if it does, we can work something out about your rent during the construction. And I guarantee the short-term pain will pay off beautifully for you once the building is open. Think of all the new customers." She was sympathetic to the disruption her projects caused but made sure to remind Kim of the long-term benefits.

"Oh. That's very ... thank you, Julie." Kim squared her shoulders and seemed to force the next words out. "But, I'm actually here about Lydia."

"Who?"

"Lydia. You know, Hudson?" She jerked her chin toward the demolished house. "That's her—that *was* her house. I ran into her on my way to my car. And, well, is she going to be okay? Does she have somewhere to go?"

Ah. That's what this was. Kim was just like everyone else. She wanted the benefit of revitalization without having to bear any of the guilt.

"Of course, Lydia Hudson. I offered Mrs. Hudson a generous price for her home."

This was true, but the woman refused to negotiate. In the end, she lost her home through the eminent domain process at pennies on the dollar. It was unfortunate and short-sighted on Lydia's part, because Julie would have gone above her initial offer if the woman had countered. But a businesswoman didn't negotiate against herself, and once Lydia made it clear she wouldn't come to the table Julie pursued other avenues to get what she wanted.

"But, she didn't sell, did she?" Kim looked confused.

"I can't get into the specifics. I'm sure you understand. But Mrs. Hudson was compensated."

At this, Sam inserted himself into the conversation. "I hear she's moving to Maryland to live with her daughter."

"See?" Julie smiled. "She'll be just fine."

Kim frowned, apparently unconvinced, but Julie was losing patience with this conversation.

"Is there anything else?" She asked, looking pointedly at the Rado watch she'd bought herself after closing her first big deal.

"I ... I guess not," the woman stammered, her cheeks red.

As Julie watched Kim hurry across the street to her car, she was reminded, as she often was, of Vera Coking. A homeowner in Atlantic City, New Jersey, Ms. Coking refused all offers for her tiny home, sandwiched between casino hotels, and successfully fought off an eminent domain proceeding through a years-long court battle. People loved pointing to the elderly widow as an example of strength and courage for the stand she took. Julie had a different takeaway from that story: Her victory was a failure of creativity on the developer's part. Julie did everything she could to get the community emotionally invested in her projects. She was generous and helpful to a fault.

So when the rare holdout like Lydia Hudson dug in to oppose her, it was Julie, not the homeowner, who garnered public sympathy. Julie understood that perception was everything.

5

GAP Mile 128.1, Clayton Falls, Pennsylvania

Bodhi covered more than twenty miles before the sun began to sink behind the mountains to the west. As he walked, his mind settled into a meditative rhythm with each light footfall—the cadence of his breath synchronized with his steps and his pack served as a grounding weight across his shoulders.

After meeting Gracie and her cat, he walked the rest of the way in solitude, save for a cluster of bicyclists who passed him headed toward Pittsburgh. By the time Clayton Falls appeared around a bend in the trail, the late afternoon light gilded the tree canopy above. The town straddled the path, having grown up around the river and rail line long before hikers and bikers claimed the route as their own.

Bodhi paused where the trail intersected with

Main Street. The town square had clearly been renovated into a postcard-perfect vision of small-town charm. A limestone courthouse with a gleaming copper dome anchored the north side, surrounded by brick storefronts with fresh paint and colorful awnings. Edison bulb string lights crisscrossed the square, ready to illuminate the evening. Each corner featured planter boxes bursting with cheerful yellow daffodils and purple crocuses, announcing the arrival of spring.

One shop, Thrown, displayed expensive-looking hand-thrown pottery glazed in subtle earth tones. Next door, the chalkboard for a farm-to-table restaurant named Forage advertised a prix fixe dinner featuring locally sourced mushrooms and heirloom vegetables. The Clayton Falls Inn dominated the east side of the square. It was a large Victorian home converted into a boutique hotel with a wraparound porch lined with rocking chairs occupied by cocktail-sipping couples dressed as if they'd magically stepped out of an outdoor clothing catalog.

Bodhi noted the main square's prosperity and the fact that it catered to visitors rather than local residents. What he was looking for would be further from the square. He adjusted his pack and continued walking. He passed through the square and followed Main Street as it descended toward the river.

The change was gradual at first—the paint a little more weathered, the sidewalks a bit more cracked, the weeds more plentiful. But by the time he crossed the rusted railroad tracks, the transformation was complete. Here was the Clayton Falls that existed beyond the carefully curated town square.

Narrow shotgun houses with sagging porches lined the potholed street. A laundromat with flickering fluorescent lights that buzzed loudly sat between a pawn shop and a check-cashing store advertising payday loans. A squat Dollar General served as the neighborhood's grocery, its parking lot dotted with cars that had seen better decades.

He turned onto a side street at random. Halfway down the block, sandwiched between two brick buildings with boarded-up windows, a hand-painted sign above a door with a hairline crack in one pane of glass identified Dot's Place. Bodhi glanced inside and saw a long counter and an open kitchen. He pushed the door open gingerly, hoping the crack wouldn't grow. A bell jangled, announcing his arrival.

The interior was shabby but clean, with curling posters on the walls and mismatched tables and chairs scattered across the floor. A yellow Formica counter lined with metal stools ran the full length of one wall. Behind it, a woman worked a flat-top grill. She glanced up at Bodhi without pausing in her movements, her spatula never breaking rhythm as she flipped crispy hash browns.

"Sit anywhere," she called. "Menus are under the napkin holders."

Bodhi chose a corner table and slipped his pack off, leaning it against the wall. He studied the laminated menu.

When the woman approached, order pad in hand, he smiled.

"Just tea for now. Hot, please."

"I've got Red Rose, no flavors or anything." She assessed him with tired eyes.

"That would be perfect, thank you."

She returned immediately with a cup of hot water and a packaged tea bag and a lemon wedge resting on the saucer. "Sugar's in the bowl. You ready to order?"

"I think so. Those hash browns don't have any egg or butter in them, right?"

She raised her left eyebrow. "You're a vegan?"

"I am."

She snorted. "You probably should have gone to Forage up on the square. They specialize in fancy plant-based meals—or so I'm told."

"I'm more of a diner guy."

Her expression softened. "The hash browns are just shredded potatoes and oil."

"Great. I'll have those."

"What else?"

He scanned the menu again. "A dish of applesauce."

She frowned and took in his attire. "You're hiking the GAP, right?"

"I am."

"Then you need some protein. I'll see what I can cobble together. I'm Dot, by the way."

"I'm Bodhi. Pleased to meet you, Dot."

While he waited for his meal, he observed the other diners—a pair of mechanics still in their coveralls with the shop name embroidered over their chest pockets, an older couple sharing a slice of pie, and a young mother who nursed a lemonade while her two tow-haired toddlers colored on paper placemats in between bites of chicken nuggets and French fries drowning in ketchup. Dot's was the quintessential neighborhood joint. A dying breed in this town, by the looks of things. He doubted any of the other customers frequented Forage.

Dot returned with a tray loaded with items that didn't appear on the menu. In addition to a heaping stack of hash browns and a mound of applesauce, there was a tower of sliced tomatoes and cucumbers, and a bowl of colorful four-bean salad.

"You need protein if you're hiking." She pointed toward the bean salad.

"You're right, I do. Thank you."

She waved his thanks away with one hand. "Let me know if you need anything."

He focused on the food before him. He was hungrier than he realized. He hadn't eaten since his send-off breakfast with Saul and Mona and their kids early in the morning. He probably should have held on to at least some of his snacks. But he was sure he could replenish his supply at the Dollar General.

Dot arrived with another cup of hot water and a fresh tea bag without his asking. "Everything all right?"

He wiped his mouth. "Better than all right. It's delicious."

She smiled. "That salad's one of my favorites. I used to have it on the menu, but I like to change things up every so often."

One of the mechanics leaned across the aisle and cracked, "Yeah, Dot refreshes her menu once a decade whether it needs it or not."

She cackled. "Pete's not wrong."

"How long have you owned this place?"

"Going on thirty years," she replied, the smile lines at the corners of her eyes crinkling. "My mom ran it before me, and her mom ran it before her."

"Was it always called Dot's Place?"

Her grin broadened at the question. "Yep. My grandma was the original Dorothy. My mom's name was Deb, and she named me Dot. That's it, just Dot."

"Your future was preordained."

"Something like that." She glanced around the room with a mixture of pride and sorrow. "We used to be busier. When the mill was still open, we'd have lines out the door for breakfast and lunch. Now"—she shrugged—"we get by."

"The town square seems to be doing well," Bodhi observed neutrally.

Her mouth tightened. "All that's new. Started about five, maybe six years ago, when some developer bought up half the buildings and got a big grant to make the place attractive to tourists. They fixed them up, cleaned up the square and made it pretty. But they doubled the rents, which pushed out most of the local businesses." She lowered her voice. "They call it revitalization, but it hasn't been kind to people who've lived here their whole lives."

Before Bodhi could respond, the door banged open and the bell jiggled wildly. A gangly teenager with wide, frightened eyes burst into the diner.

"I need help!" he shouted, scanning the room frantically. "Joey's not breathing right!"

Bodhi jumped up. "I'm a doctor."

"He's in the alley. Hurry!"

Bodhi grabbed his pack and followed the boy out the door and around the corner. In the narrow space between Dot's and the adjacent abandoned building, a young man lay sprawled on the cracked pavement. His fair skin was tinged blue and his breathing was shallow and erratic.

Kneeling beside him, Bodhi recognized the signs immediately—pinpoint pupils, respiratory depression, unresponsiveness. He reached into his pack and retrieved one of the naloxone doses Saul had insisted he take.

"How long has he been like this?" Bodhi asked the teen, who shifted his weight from foot to foot.

"I dunno. Five minutes, less maybe? We were just hanging out, smoking, and then he started nodding off."

Bodhi placed the young man in the recovery position on his side. "What's his name?"

"Joey. Joey Alton."

"Joey." Bodhi said the name in a firm, insistent voice as he ground his knuckles into the man's sternum in an effort to rouse him. "Joey, can you hear me?"

No response. Bodhi administered the nasal spray and waited, watching the shallow, slow rise and fall of Joey's chest.

Joey's breathing gradually deepened. His eyelids flickered, then opened. Confusion gave way to recognition as he focused on the teenager peering down at him.

"Damn it, Camden," he mumbled. "Why'd you have to—"

"You weren't breathing right!" Camden shot back. "I thought you were dying."

A small crowd had gathered at the mouth of the

alley. Dot pushed her way through the cluster of people, her face tight with concern.

"Joey Alton," she said, clucking her tongue. "Your mom's gonna have a fit."

"Please don't tell her, Dot," Joey pleaded, attempting to sit up. Bodhi placed a steadying hand on his shoulder.

"Take it slow," he advised. "The Narcan blocks the opiates, but it can wear off before they do. You need go to a hospital."

Joey shook his head emphatically. "No hospital. Can't afford it."

"What about the clinic up in Clarksville?" Camden suggested.

"That closed last year," Dot informed him grimly.

Bodhi helped Joey into a seated position with his back against the wall. The young man was thin but not emaciated, his clothes worn but clean. Despite Saul's warnings about homelessness and addiction on the trail, Joey was clearly a local.

"You live around here?" Bodhi asked.

Joey looked away. "Sort of. Been staying with friends since I got evicted."

"He was the assistant manager at the hardware store on the square," Dot supplied. "Lost his job when they turned it into a sip and paint craft shop. Then his rent went up. You can guess the rest."

He could. Down on his luck, with no opportunities on the horizon, Joey had decided to escape his troubles in one of the few ways available to him.

"There's nothing here for guys like us anymore," Camden said. There was a bitter edge to his young voice. "You gotta have money to spend in those tourist places, or you gotta have money to open one. If you don't have either, you're screwed."

Joey nodded his agreement. "I've been applying everywhere. Even in Pittsburgh. I haven't gotten a single interview or a call back. I started using to take the edge off. Just sometimes." He studied his shoes. "Then it got to be more than sometimes."

Bodhi understood both Joey's immediate crisis and the systemic one it pointed to. This story wasn't unique to Clayton Falls. He'd seen variations of it in Vermont and in Florida, small communities, once overlooked, where so-called progress created winners and losers with little, if any, middle ground.

"You need to rest," Bodhi told Joey. "And you *really* should seek medical attention. As I said, the spray's effect is temporary."

Joey nodded without conviction, and Bodhi knew his advice would go unheeded. He reached into his pack again and retrieved the remaining doses of the spray.

"Do you know how to use these?" he asked Camden, who nodded.

"They taught us in health class last year."

"Good. Keep them with you." Bodhi handed over the doses, then turned back to Joey. "This isn't a solution. Just a second chance."

"What am I supposed to do with a second chance around here?" Joey asked the question with genuine bewilderment.

Bodhi thought of Gracie and her cat, of Dot's struggling diner, and of the gleaming shops in the town square that might as well have been in another world.

"First, you survive," he said finally.

The onlookers drifted away, and Camden settled on the ground next to Joey with his back against the brick wall. A Black woman wearing blue scrubs under a cheerful red coat walked toward them and addressed Bodhi.

"I'm a nurse practitioner. I can stay with them for a bit. And maybe convince Joey to get checked out."

He smiled in relief. "Thank you."

She placed a hand on Bodhi's arm. "No, thank you. You probably saved his life."

"You'd have done the same."

"Rae," Dot said to the nurse practitioner, "You be sure to stop in for a slice of pie and a cup of coffee on the house before you head home for the night."

Rae nodded.

Dot and Bodhi walked back toward the diner as the shadows lengthened and dusk fell around them.

"Joey was always a good kid, but he's floundering."

"I hope he finds his way out of his troubles." He couldn't help but think of Joey's question—what would he do with a second chance in a town like this?

"Where are you staying tonight?" Dot asked, pulling him out of his thoughts.

"I haven't decided yet. Is there a motel nearby?"

She chortled. "The Inn's your only official option, and they charge more per night than my weekly take. But I've got a spare room upstairs. It's nothing fancy, but it's clean. I'll even throw in breakfast."

He didn't hesitate to accept the offer. "Thank you."

He washed up in the restroom before returning to

his table to finish his meal. As he scrubbed his hands, he reflected on the stark disparity between the revitalized square and the rest of the town. The town's charming facade shielded visitors from the harsh reality. But the despair and neglect lurked just under the surface, as real as ever.

6

Union Hill

Rory set up the camera to transfer the photos to the editing software on her laptop. Then she crossed to the kitchen and poured a flute of champagne.

Her regular indulgence in sparkling wine was one of the few vestiges of her former life. She smiled faintly at the memory of her Great-Aunt Beatrice defending her habit to the rest of the family a few years ago.

"Why should she wait for a special occasion? She could get mowed down in the street tomorrow." She'd turned toward Rory and said, "You drink your bubbly, love. The rest of you could take a lesson."

Beatrice had gone on to point out that she always used her good china, even when she ate alone, and spritzed herself with Chanel No. 5 perfume daily, even if the only activity she had planned was to mop the kitchen floor. Rory laughed lightly at the recollection. Great-Aunt Beatrice got it.

She settled into her plush criss-cross platform chair and pulled up her message thread to pass the time while she waited for the images to transfer. She immediately wished she hadn't.

Tripp had texted yet again. When she saw his name, she wrinkled her nose involuntarily, then scanned the message with a knot in her stomach. While gallery shows always involved a lot of coordination and confirmation of details, Tripp was involving himself in the nitty-gritty in a way that gallery owners seldom did. As if he was using the show as an excuse to contact her—repeatedly.

She blew out a breath, ruffling her hair, and opened the text:

> Not sure you listened to my messages. Having trouble generating buzz for show. Had a brilliant thought. How about a series of nude self-portraits? A way to show the woman behind the camera. With your background, would be a smash.

Rory's stomach roiled as a wave of disgust washed over her. She wasn't stupid. She'd known from the beginning that a large part of the reason Tripp had agreed to hang her show was that she'd been a Next Icon contest winner a dozen years ago. A seventeen-year-old fashion runway model turned supermodel was the stuff of dreams, masturbatory and otherwise.

But she wasn't that same girl anymore. She'd gone on to earn a degree in photography and had carved out a career for herself as a serious photographer in the hope that her body of work would eventually eclipse her physical body. Sometimes it did.

Apparently not this time. Now, despite the reputation she'd built, she was fielding unsolicited text requests for nudes. Not that she had anything against nude photography or nude self-portraits. Plenty of photographers—fine art, commercial, and photojournalistic—worked with nude models.

But Rory didn't, and Tripp knew it. He'd only felt comfortable making the request because once upon a time she'd been a glorified clothes hanger. And possibly because of her connection to Lucas. At this thought, her anger flared hotter.

She took a swig of champagne and waited for the fuzzy burn to hit the back of her throat. She continued to sip the drink and watched the sun slip lower in the sky. Once she had her temper in hand, she refilled her glass, picked up the phone, and called Tripp's number.

He answered on the second ring, rush hour traffic noises behind him—idling buses, honking horns, and sirens.

"Aurora, it's good to hear from you." His voice was warm, almost intimate, as he greeted her. Then his timbre shifted, becoming petulant. "I was beginning to think you were ignoring me."

"I was in the middle of a session when you called." She kept her tone neutral.

He cut to the chase. "Have you had a chance to consider my proposal? It's a surefire way to get the attention of the art world."

She made a noncommittal "hmm" sound before

she said, "I want to make sure I understand it. Text has no tone, you know, so I thought a conversation would be in order."

"Of course," he said, sounding eager. "We could even meet in person if you want. I'll come to you."

The last thing she wanted was Tripp showing up on her doorstep.

She shut the idea down instantly. "A phone conversation is more than sufficient."

"Okay. Well, it's pretty straightforward: You include some nude self-portraits in the exhibit. The art world goes wild."

"But my body has no bearing on the theme of the show. The exhibit is titled *Push/Pull* because it documents the displacement of people and businesses along the trail who've been pushed out as part of the effort to attract tourists and more lucrative businesses. Your idea would detract from the installation's impact, not add to it."

He protested, undeterred. "Imagine the attention it would generate."

Had he even glanced at the images she'd sent him? Did he have any idea what the show was about?

"My answer is no." She spoke firmly but calmly.

"Hold on a second. I'm going to duck into a coffee shop where it's quieter." She listened as the street noise faded and a bell jangled. He spoke again in a muffled tone. "That's a problem."

"Oh?"

"Yeah. Why are you making such a big deal out of this?"

"I don't want to do it. You asked; I answered." She reminded herself that no was a complete sentence.

"Lucas told me you would definitely do it."

Lucas. She knew it. She clutched the stem of her glass and steadied her voice. "He isn't authorized to speak for me."

"Well, I thought he'd know. So I ...," he trailed off.

"You what?"

He cleared his throat. "I already sent out the press release."

"Excuse me?" Hot anger surged through her chest and her heart thumped.

"What's the problem? You used to take your clothes off all the time. Just take a few shots—make them as artsy as you want. We'll hang them in the back corner. They won't take away from the impact of the exhibit."

"I said no."

Tripp sighed heavily. "Well, Rory, I don't know what to tell you. My hands are tied. If you're not gonna do it, then I'll have to cancel the show."

"What?" The word shot from her mouth like a missile.

"I can't send out another release that says, 'No, as it turns out, there won't be a series of nudes of the photographer.' I'll look like a joke."

It didn't seem to matter to him that *she* would look like a joke if she inserted nude self-portraits in her exhibit about economic displacement. But there was no point arguing with Tripp.

"Then I guess the show's canceled."

She ended the call over his blustering.

After a moment, she stepped out onto the balcony with her champagne, filled her lungs with cool evening air, and blinked back tears of rage. Then she leaned on the railing to look down at the street below. Fairy lights twinkled from the storefronts and lamp posts. Acoustic music floated up from the open windows of the coffeehouse. Across the street, she spotted Julie at a table on the bistro's patio. She sat alone, nursing a glass of wine and studying the menu.

Rory downed the rest of her drink and rushed back inside. She couldn't do anything about Tripp and the show right now, but she could ask Julie why the hell she'd made a lifelong resident of the town homeless.

She ran a brush through her tangle of white-blonde hair and swiped a lipstick over her mouth. Then she threw a soft, snowy cashmere shawl over her uniform of fitted black tee shirt and jeans. Appearances mattered to Julie. And Rory knew how to play this game.

7

———————

Julie swirled her glass of cabernet sauvignon, savoring the complex notes of blackberry, coffee, and cedar as she studied the bistro's menu. The crispy duck confit with wild mushroom risotto caught her eye as the perfect celebratory meal. Today marked a significant milestone in the Allegheny Luxury Lofts project, and she intended to toast her success properly, even if she dined alone.

The lights strung across the bistro's patio bathed the cobblestone courtyard in a warm glow. As Julie swept her gaze over the lit-up boutiques and restaurants that lined Railroad Way, glittering like gems in the dark, a rush of pride washed over her.

Five years ago, this stretch had been a sad collection of vacant storefronts and crumbling buildings. The structures were neglected relics of a long-ago era when the railroad and coal had brought prosperity to these hills. Forget vacationers, the residents couldn't wait to escape. The Great Allegheny Passage had brought new life to the region and she—Julie Mason —had seized the opportunity with both hands.

Now, the street hummed with activity. Tourists and transplants mingled, their laughter carrying in the night. Soft music rose on the cool spring breeze. This was her vision realized: a revitalized Union Hill, reborn as a destination rather than a pit stop on the way to nowhere.

Her server approached the table, but before Julie could order, movement across the street caught her eye. A tall, willowy figure with distinctive icy blonde hair descended the exterior staircase of the renovated mercantile building—her first successful conversion project. Julie recognized Rory instantly. The former supermodel was unmistakable even at a distance.

Rory glanced at her and crossed the street with a purposeful stride, heading directly toward the bistro's courtyard. Julie straightened in her chair, oddly pleased. Rory Westin was exactly the type of resident she'd hoped to attract when she'd begun investing in Union Hill—creative, sophisticated, cosmopolitan. The photographer had biked the Great Allegheny Passage from the C&O Canal Towpath connector two Aprils ago. After a weekend stay in Union Hill, she'd promptly fallen in love with the town and returned to Washington just long enough to pack her belongings before relocating to Julie's first residential property.

"I'll give you a few more minutes," the server said, noting Rory's approach. He melted into the background.

Rory slipped into the chair across from Julie, her snow-white cashmere wrap luminous in the dim light. Up close, the photographer's high, curved cheekbones were taut, her muscles tensed, almost as if she were going into battle. July couldn't imagine why.

"What a lovely surprise," she said warmly, gesturing to her wine. "Let me order you a glass. The cabernet is excellent."

"No, thank you," Rory replied, her voice cool and measured. "I'm not staying."

Something in her tone made Julie set down her glass. "Is everything all right with the apartment? If there's a maintenance issue—"

"This isn't about my apartment," Rory cut in. "It's about Lydia Hudson's home."

Julie blinked slowly and tried to hide her surprise at being ambushed for the second time about Lydia Hudson. She couldn't imagine Rory knew the woman, let alone cared about the situation. Then she remembered the photographer across the road, sitting with Lydia as she watched her house crumble to the ground.

"I see," she said carefully. "You were at the demolition site today."

"I was documenting it. For Mrs. Hudson." Her tone held a challenge.

Bristling, Julie sipped her wine before responding. She used the moment to collect her thoughts and form a tactful response. "It's unfortunate Lydia had to be relocated. Unfortunate, but necessary for the town's growth."

"Necessary?" Rory's cornflower blue eyes flashed. "It was necessary to force a woman out of her family home? A home that's stood for over a century, a home that her grandparents built with their own hands?"

"The town council determined—"

"The town council is stacked with your business associates," Rory interrupted. "Let's not pretend this was some democratic process. You wanted that property for your luxury lofts, and when Lydia wouldn't sell, you used eminent domain as a weapon."

Julie's skin heated as a flush crept up her neck, but she maintained a neutral expression. This was far from the first time she'd faced criticism for her development projects, although it *was* the first she'd been challenged by someone who so directly benefited from them.

"I understand it looks harsh from the outside," Julie said, her voice even. "But you don't know what it was like before. Union Hill was dying, Rory. The young people left in droves because there were no jobs. Buildings literally crumbled from neglect. The tax base couldn't support basic services." She leaned forward. "My projects create economic opportunity. The Allegheny Luxury Lofts will bring construction jobs, service positions, increased tourism—"

"At what cost?" Rory challenged. "And for whose benefit? Certainly not for people like Lydia."

Julie's professional smile faltered. "Not everyone will benefit equally in the short term, that's true. Change is difficult. But in the long run, a rising tide lifts all boats."

Rory scoffed. "A rising tide drowns those who can't afford a boat. People aren't abstract economic units, Julie. They're human beings with histories and memories. They have emotional attachments to their homes. Did you even talk to Lydia before you decided to bulldoze her home?"

The accusation stung because it contained a

kernel of truth. Julie had sent lawyers and real estate appraisers to the Hudson home bearing offers. But, no, she'd never sat down with Lydia herself.

"It isn't personal," Julie insisted. "It's business."

"It's personal to Lydia. It's personal to everyone being pushed out of their homes and businesses." Rory's voice rose slightly, drawing glances from diners at nearby tables. "Do you have any idea what it's like to be displaced? To have your entire life upended because someone more powerful decides your home, your community, your footprint, isn't valuable enough to exist?"

The irony of the situation wasn't lost on Julie. She gestured toward the square. "You wouldn't even be here if not for the development you're criticizing. That studio apartment you love so much? It used to be a derelict storage space above a failing mercantile store. The owner was drowning in debt and about to lose the building to the bank. I paid him a fair price and created something viable. I displaced him for people like *you*."

Rory didn't flinch. "And I pay you a substantial rent for that space. But I wouldn't have moved here if I'd known the cost also included pushing out lifelong residents."

"That's a convenient moral position to take after the fact," Julie shot back, her patience wearing thin. "What would you have me do now? Return the old buildings back to their original state? Should I close the bistro, the boutiques, the coffee shop? Tell the tourists to go elsewhere? Because that's the alternative. Without investment, this town would be gasping for breath, like so many other dying towns that haven't harnessed the potential of the GAP."

The air between them was thick with tension.

Julie took another sip of wine, feeling a headache forming at her temples. She genuinely believed in what she was doing—revitalizing her hometown, creating opportunity in the place of stagnation. Why couldn't people like Rory see beyond the immediate disruption to the long-term good?

When Rory remained silent, Julie tried again in a gentler tone. "Look, I grew up in Union Hill. I left for college and stayed away for twenty years because there was nothing to come back to. I'm trying to change that. To create a place where people want to live, work, and visit. Is that really so terrible?"

Rory's expression softened, the tight line of her jaw relaxing. "Your intentions may be good, but your methods are heartless. There are ways to develop communities that include existing residents rather than displacing them. Affordable housing set-asides. Local hiring requirements. Rent control. Business incubators for local entrepreneurs. Investment in social programs geared to the community, not just events to attract visitors." She shook her head. "But I suppose that would mean more effort and, presumably, less profit."

Julie stiffened. "You don't know the first thing about my profit margins or the work I've put into improving this town—for everyone."

Rory slid a knowing eye over Julie's couture outfit, two-carat ring, and designer bag and smirked.

Julie resisted the urge to squirm under the scrutiny. Instead she forced a smile and changed the subject. Everyone loved talking about themselves. Especially the artsy types.

"How are the preparations coming for your exhibition in Pittsburgh? *Push/Pull*, I believe it is. Landing a showing at the Hot Metal Gallery is quite an achievement."

Rory's nostrils flared. "It's been canceled."

"What? Why?" Julie asked, genuinely surprised. "I thought it was opening next week."

"Creative differences," Rory said flatly. "The gallery owner wanted to take the show in a direction I wasn't comfortable with."

Julie sensed there was more to the story but knew better than to press. "I'm sorry to hear that. Your work is exceptional. It deserves to be seen."

Rory stood abruptly, adjusting her wrap around her shoulders. "Well, it seems we don't always get what we deserve."

The pointed comment hung in the air like a raindrop, trembling on a branch, about to fall. Then Rory turned on her heel.

Julie watched her stride away, the white cashmere shawl fluttering behind her as she crossed the courtyard and disappeared into her building. For a long moment, Julie sat perfectly still, the weight of the confrontation wedged in her stomach like a brick.

She chafed at being cast as the villain. If anything, she was the hometown hero, returning to save Union Hill from the slow death of irrelevance. She created jobs, attracted investment, and breathed life into abandoned buildings. In her own way, she was an artist, too, molding the town to her vision. So why did Rory's accusations unsettle her?

If she were honest, she knew the answer. Rory's points had struck a nerve because they touched on doubts that plagued her in unguarded moments.

Had she been too ruthless in pursuing her goals? Could she have found a way to include Lydia and others like her in the new Union Hill she was creating?

No. Julie brushed the thoughts aside like cobwebs. Growth inevitably entailed growing pains. But the results would vindicate her approach. Union Hill would thrive again—a new town designed for a new era.

She signaled for the server.

"I'm ready to order now," she chirped, her smile firmly back in place. "The duck confit, please. And another glass of the cabernet."

As he retreated, she turned her gaze toward the string of fairy lights illuminating Railroad Way. Beyond them, in the distance, she could just make out the faint silhouette of the construction equipment still positioned at what had been the Hudson property. Tomorrow, workers would clear away the debris dig the foundation for the Allegheny Luxury Lofts.

Change, she reminded herself, was inevitable. Those who couldn't adapt would be left behind. It was simply the way the world worked.

But when she raised her glass again, the wine tasted bitter.

8

———————

Clayton Falls

The first rays of early sunlight filtered through the thin curtains and fell across Bodhi's face. He opened his eyes and blinked, momentarily disoriented by the unfamiliar surroundings. Then he remembered. He was in the guest room above Dot's. The sparsely furnished bedroom had a simple, almost monastic quality—a twin bed with a metal frame, one wooden chair in the corner, and a small dresser that held a tray with a pitcher of water and a drinking glass. If he squinted, he could almost believe he was at a meditation retreat center. He smiled softly. Dot should market the place that way. She'd have to beat off the would-be meditators and yogis with a stick.

He sat up and rolled first his neck, then his shoulders, working out the kinks from the previous day's long hike. Outside, a robin chirped, welcoming the spring morning with its song.

Bodhi threw back the handmade quilt and padded to the chair where he'd rested his backpack before settling into sleep. He unrolled his thin travel mat and moved through his morning yoga routine—cat-cow, downward dog, the warrior poses, forward fold, mountain pose, and, finally, extended child's pose, each *asana* flowing into the next like water. As he moved, his muscles warmed and loosened and his mind shed the last residue of sleep.

He arranged himself in the lotus position on his mat and transitioned into his medication practice. He focused on his breath, taking note of each inhalation and exhalation. Thoughts arose—reflections on yesterday's encounter with Gracie, concern over Joey's addiction, curiosity about what the future held for Dot and her town. He observed them, then invited them to drift away like clouds moving across the sky as he returned to his breath.

Twenty minutes later, he opened his eyes, his mind quiet and at peace. He rolled up the mat and returned it to its bag before gathering his toiletries and a change of clothes. He walked lightly down the hallway to the shared bathroom. The pipes groaned when he turned the shower knob, but the water was hot and the pressure was strong.

After toweling off, he brushed his teeth, combed through his damp curls, and dressed in lightweight hiking pants and a moisture-wicking shirt. When he returned to the bedroom, he folded his sleeping clothes and tucked them into his backpack along with the toiletry case. He moved with unhurried efficiency.

After smoothing the quilt and plumping the pillow, he surveyed the room to confirm he was leaving it as he'd found it. Then he shouldered his pack and descended the narrow staircase, each step creaking under the weight of his boots.

The scents of coffee, French toast, and frying bacon wafted up to greet him. The diner was already half-full. A few people nodded in his direction, curious and welcoming. He heard Joey's name and understood that the small-town grapevine was doing its job.

As he passed by the counter, Dot called out to him from behind the grill, raising her voice to be heard over the sizzle of bacon in a cast-iron skillet. "Morning, Doc!"

"Good morning, Dot." His efforts to get her to call him Bodhi instead of Dr. King had been futile. 'Doc' was progress.

"There's a baked oatmeal finishing up in the oven for you. I'll be out with your tea in a flash. Grab the paper from the counter while you wait."

A copy of *The Allegheny Herald* lay folded on the counter next to the cash register. Bodhi took it to the same corner table he'd occupied the night before. He skimmed the front page—local politics, a debate over school funding, an upcoming strawberry festival. Flipping the page, his gaze snagged on a black-and-white photograph that took up the top half. He studied it.

An old man sat on the porch of a modest house. Light filtered through the porch's weathered railings, casting striped shadows across his lined face. His strong, gnarled hands gripped the knees of his khaki work pants. Behind him, a window reflected the shape of a hulking excavator across the street. The photograph highlighted decades of grueling work and hinted at a harbinger of change—or was it doom?

The caption read: "Edward Kovalic, 86, the last resident of Company Row, reflects on a lifetime in coal country as demolition begins on neighboring homes. Photo by Aurora Westin."

An article below the photograph focused on a new exhibit at the Western Trail History Center outside Union Hill, titled *Vanishing Coal Country: A Visual Record.* It quoted both the photographer and the center's director:

"'These company homes aren't just buildings. Think of them as a living record of the coal industry, the miners who settled here and built these towns, or a living archive of our region's industrial heritage,' explains photographer Aurora Westin. 'Each home holds generations of stories to be preserved, even as the region moves forward in a new direction.'"

"Professor Evan Jeffries, director of the Western Trail History Center, praises Westin's work for its 'unflinching honesty and deep empathy.' 'These photographs force us to confront difficult questions about progress and preservation in communities like ours,' Jeffries notes. 'They remind us that history isn't just in the past—we're making it with every decision about what we keep and what we discard.'"

Bodhi studied the photograph again. There was a quiet dignity in the man's face. The composition was somehow at once haunting and hopeful.

A ceramic mug of steaming tea appeared at his elbow, followed by a bowl of golden-brown baked oatmeal topped with diced apples dusted with cinnamon.

"Rory's got an eye, doesn't she?" Dot said, nodding toward the newspaper as she lifted a small pitcher of what appeared to be milk over his oatmeal.

Bodhi looked up. "She certainly does."

"She had a whole series in the paper a few months back. Took pictures of all the old miners and mill workers she could find. Asked them their stories, too." Dot caught him looking at the pitcher. "Don't worry. Joey's mum—Wendy Alton—works at the natural food store on the square. She brought over a carton of soy milk for you."

"She didn't need to do that," he protested.

She raised an eyebrow. "You saved her numbskull of a son's life. I think a carton of milk is the least she can do." She poured it over the oatmeal and then placed it on the table beside his tea.

He jerked his chin toward the photograph and article. "Is this series on display at the history center now?"

She nodded. "Yep. When Professor Evans saw the series, he approached Rory about expanding it into a permanent exhibit. The whole thing caused a bit of a stir in the string of towns between here and Union Hill. Some folks thought she made the region seem backward or downtrodden, but some of us were glad someone was paying attention."

"It must be a difficult balancing act to acknowledge the past without getting trapped in it."

"Don't know that there's much balancing happening." Dot glanced at the photograph again. "They're tearing down the whole Company Row to put in a tech incubator. The promise is it'll bring jobs, but they sure won't be for the families from Company Row."

No, he imagined they wouldn't be.

She gestured toward the bowl. "Go on, try it."

He dug his spoon into the oatmeal and took a mouthful. The hot grains were sweetened with maple syrup and studded with walnuts, apples and dried cherries, and several spices. He could make out cinnamon, ginger, and cardamom. "It's delicious."

Dot beamed. "I thought so, too. I had a bowl myself to try it. Even used the soy milk." She lowered her voice conspiratorially. "Don't tell my regulars, but I think I'm gonna add it to the menu. No need to announce that it's vegan."

He chuckled and Dot bustled off to refill several coffee mugs and deliver a plate of home fries and eggs to Camden, who turned to wave to Bodhi at her direction. By the time she returned to check on him, his bowl was half empty.

"You must like it," she said in a satisfied tone.

"I never lie," he told her. Then gestured toward the paper. "There's a line at the end of the article that mentions an upcoming exhibition in Pittsburgh. I know the gallery. That's a big deal."

"Her first time for a major gallery show, from what I hear. Rory's been published in magazines and such, but this is different. Folks around here are pretty excited for her, even the ones who don't much like her subject matter." Dot replaced his mug of tea with a fresh one. "She lives just up the trail in Union Hill. Can't miss her if you're heading that way. Tall, striking woman. White-blonde hair. Looks like she stepped off the cover of a fashion magazine. I suppose because she did."

"Pardon?"

"She used to be a model." Dot's eyes narrowed and she tilted her head. "You single?"

"I am."

"Into women?"

"I am," he repeated, amusement crinkling the corners of his eyes.

"Well then," Dot said, letting the implication hang in the air.

Before she could elaborate, he added gently, "I'm on a solo journey at the moment. Seeking clarity, not companionship."

To his relief, she didn't press. Instead, she nodded her understanding. "Sometimes you've got to get your own house in order before inviting anyone else in."

"Something like that," Bodhi agreed.

His last relationship had been with Bette, the chief of police of a small town in Illinois. They'd maintained a long-distance connection for many years, finding a rhythm of visits and video calls that suited them both. But when Bette retired and decided to move to Oregon to be near her sister, she'd made the unilateral decision that the new, longer, distance was insurmountable.

Bodhi hadn't argued. He understood her reasoning. In some ways, he was relieved. They ended their relationship on good terms. Still, it left him contemplative about what he wanted from his relationships, his work, his life. These were the questions that had set him out on the trail in search of answers.

He finished his breakfast and unfolded the map

he carried. Studying it alongside the trail guide, he traced his finger along the Great Allegheny Passage.

"Planning today's journey?" Dot asked, appearing at his shoulder.

"Yes. I'm deciding how far to go."

"Weather's supposed to be good. Clear and cool." She pointed to a spot on the map. "Union Hill's about forty miles up. It's a pretty little town. On the leading edge of our regional rejuvenation, as the chamber of commerce likes to say."

Bodhi aimed for roughly twenty miles a day. It was a reasonable, sustainable distance.

"That's a good goal for tomorrow," he told her. "What's halfway between here and there?"

She waved her hand. "Eh, Clarksville. Not much there, I'm afraid. But my cousin's youngest boy has a burger joint. Stop in and grab a bite. Tell him Aunt Dot sent you. He'll find you somewhere to lay your head for the night."

"Where exactly is the burger place?"

"Like I said, there's not much there. You'll find it."

"Okay, then."

"But then, you'll aim for Union Hill tomorrow?"

He decided he would. "Union Hill it is."

She smiled. "If you get there before dinner, try the bistro on Railroad Way. It's pricey, but they'll have your plant-based dishes. And you might even run into our local photographer. A solo journey doesn't have to mean complete solitude, does it?"

Bodhi thanked her for the recommendation without commenting on her obvious matchmaking. He settled his bill for the meal and the room, added a generous tip, and thanked Dot warmly once again for her kindness and hospitality.

She surprised him and, judging by her expression, herself by enveloping him in a brief hug when he stood to shrug into his backpack. Then she shooed him out the door.

The morning air was cool, but it held the promise of warmth. Across the street from Dot's Place, young green shoots peeked out from a small vegetable garden ringed by a chain-link fence. Even this tired part of town held signs of spring, life, and renewal to inspire gratitude.

He oriented himself toward the trail and set out on the day's journey, syncing his breath to his footfalls. Before long, his thoughts wandered from the trail to return to the photograph of Edward Kovalic and the photographer who saw the truth so clearly. What had the professor said about her work? He called up the quote from his memory: "unflinching honesty and deep empathy."

The exhibit sounded impactful. Maybe he'd detour to the Western Trail History Center to see it for himself. Despite Dot's good-natured hints, he was more interested in the photographs than the photographer.

PART II

People only see what they are prepared to see.

— RALPH WALDO EMERSON,
AMERICAN TRANSCENDENTALIST

*It's not what we look at that matters, it's what
we see.*

— HENRY DAVID THOREAU,
AMERICAN TRANSCENDENTALIST

9

———————

Union Hill

The Pilates studio occupied what had once been a milliner's shop on Railroad Way. The restored original tin ceiling gleamed above the new bamboo flooring and the exposed brick walls had been painted a soft, creamy white. Morning light streamed through the plate-glass windows, illuminating the six Reformer machines as well as Rory and the five other women who lay on them.

"Extend through your heels, ladies. Find length in your spine," Lissa, the instructor, encouraged as she moved among them. "Now, control the return. Slowly, slowly."

Rory focused on her breath as she pulled the carriage back to its resting position. The familiar burn in her core and thighs anchored her, momentarily distracting her from the whirlwind of anxious thoughts that had been her constant companion since the previous day. Lydia's demolished home, Tripp's gross behavior, the cancellation of her first big gallery show, and the unsatisfying conversation with Julie all swirled in her mind, a constant intrusion.

As she moved through the exercises, her gaze drifted to the storefronts visible across the street. The plant bar offered a propagation station and a sustainable gardening workshop. Next door, a fiber artist spun yarn that she then custom hand-dyed. Next, was the ancient grains bakery. And the last shop on that side of the block was a co-op that offered toothpaste tablets, refillable soaps and detergents, and waxed wraps to replace your plastic wrap and sandwich bags —all in service of a greener lifestyle, provided you could swing the annual membership fee and the refill prices.

Her stomach twisted, not from stretching, but from sour guilt. Wasn't she part of this transformation? Didn't she benefit from it? She paid premium rent for her apartment/studio space and could afford these classes, those shops, that upscale coffeehouse that had replaced the Union Hill diner, and the organic groceries at the new market. How different was she, really, from the tourists and transplants Julie was so eager to attract? No different at all, she answered herself bitterly. Julie was right about that much.

"And release," Lissa's voice pulled her back to the present. "Beautiful work today, everyone. See you on Wednesday!"

As the class dispersed, Rory wiped down her machine and collected her water bottle and towel.

She'd moved to Union Hill seeking authenticity—an escape from the artifice of her modeling career and the pretentiousness of the D.C. art scene. Yet here she was, surrounded by the same carefully curated aesthetic in a different, more rustic setting.

"You were somewhere else today," Lissa observed as Rory gathered her things. "Everything okay?"

"I was distracted," she admitted. "I have a lot on my mind."

Lissa nodded sympathetically, tucking a strand of bright pink hair behind her ear. "Heard about your gallery show. That's rough."

News traveled fast in Union Hill. Rory shouldn't have been surprised. "Word's out already?"

"Julie mentioned it at the five am class."

Rory groaned. Why had she told Julie, of all people?

"Want my advice?" Lissa continued, "Put it firmly in the rearview and move on. Pittsburgh has other galleries."

"Thanks," she managed.

If only it was that easy. Tripp was an undeniable slimebag, but Hot Metal was one of the most prestigious contemporary art spaces in western Pennsylvania. Walking away felt like a significant career setback. Probably because it was.

She said goodbye to Lissa, pulled her fleece jacket over her head, and pushed through the door. Before her feet hit the pavement, her phone was vibrating in her thigh pocket of her leggings. Again. She ignored it. Tripp had been calling all morning, and she had no intention of talking to him.

Ember + Bean sat on the corner diagonally across

from the Pilates studio. The coffee shop's outdoor tables were crowded with hearty, caffeinated souls ready to embrace spring despite the temperature hovering in the low fifties. Rory joined the line inside and inhaled deeply. She loved the intoxicating, homey aroma of fresh coffee and baked goods. If someone bottled it as a perfume, she'd adopt it as her signature scent.

"Well, if it isn't our local celebrity!"

The warm, raspy voice belonged to Diana Mercer, seated at her usual table in the corner. Union Hill's former police chief motioned Rory over.

"Celebrity seems like a stretch," Rory replied after she ordered her usual and joined Diana at the corner table. "What are you talking about?"

"*The Herald* ran a feature on your *Vanishing Coal Country* exhibit this morning *and* they mentioned your upcoming show in Pittsburgh. On top of all that, Evan Jeffries sang your praises, and he's a well-known curmudgeon." Diana waved toward a booth on the other side of the small coffee shop. "Aaron read the entire article aloud to me, not to mention the rest of the patrons."

As if summoned, Aaron appeared at Rory's elbow, newspaper in hand. His eager smile and warm brown eyes were boyish, despite the fact that he was closing in on thirty-five. In truth, he reminded Rory of an overgrown puppy. A golden retriever or maybe a chocolate lab.

"Thought you'd want to have a copy," he enthused, thrusting the paper toward her. "They used the Kovalic portrait. It looks amazing even in the smudgy newspaper ink."

"Thanks." Rory took it from him, trying to hide her discomfort.

She and Aaron had dated briefly—very briefly—when she first moved to Union Hill. After three casual dinners and one awkward morning after, she gently informed him that they were better as friends. The situation wasn't helped by the fact that he had an on-again, off-again girlfriend, Sadie. He and Sadie had definitely been *off* when Rory arrived in town, but they were *on* now. And Sadie was the type to hold a grudge.

Proving the point, she appeared beside Aaron. "Come on, babe. We're going to be late opening the shop."

Sadie managed the local outdoor gear shop, where Aaron also worked. She jangled a set of keys at him for emphasis before turning to give Rory a tight smile. "Congrats on the news coverage."

"Thanks. Although I haven't read it yet," Rory said, hoping the measured response would head off any ugliness.

No such luck.

"Well, don't get too comfortable with the attention," Sadie said with a lightness that didn't quite mask the edge in her voice. "Small-town fame is fleeting. Last month it was Val Taylor's blue-ribbon jam at the county fair. Next month, it'll be that trainer in the valley who has a corgi competing at the dog show."

Aaron shot Rory an apologetic look as he hustled his girlfriend out of the shop. "You're right. We should get going. See you around, Rory."

Before they were out the door, Diana was chuckling. "I see Sadie's still threatened by you."

"She just thrives on drama," Rory murmured, glancing down at the newspaper.

There was her photograph of Edward Kovalic. Despite herself, she had to agree with Aaron: the composition and the contrast of light and dark was as powerful in newsprint as it had been in her viewfinder.

Before she could read the article, a conversation from the next table caught her attention.

"—going to be the biggest development yet. Mason says they're bringing in an anchor tenant from Pittsburgh. Some tech company looking for a satellite office with 'rural charm.'"

Rory peeked at the speaker from under her eyelashes. She didn't recognize the middle-aged man in a polo shirt.

He leaned toward his companion. "It's a prime location, right where the trail meets the river."

His friend nodded. "Heard they're calling it the Riverview Exchange. Mixed-use with luxury condos on the upper floors. Starting at what, half a million?"

"More, I think. Mason's got a waiting list already. You should get on it if you have any interest at all." This last bit was said in a hushed voice, barely above a whisper.

Rory's pulse sped up. The patch of land where the trail met the river was currently a scrubby field where local kids played pickup soccer, people walked their dogs, and a group of feisty Italian-American retirees played bocce and drank red table wine from coffee mugs. The Patch, as everyone called it, was one of the few undeveloped spaces left in town, a casual community gathering spot.

"Rory? Your dirty latte's up." The barista's voice broke through her thoughts.

She collected her drink, mulling over what she'd just overheard. Another Julie Mason project, another piece of Union Hill transformed into something unrecognizable to its longtime residents.

Diana peered through her yellow-tinted glasses at Rory as she returned to the table. "You look like someone just peed in your coffee. You're not letting Sadie get to you, are you?"

"Of course not," Rory scoffed, sliding into the chair across from the former chief. "Have you heard about Julie's plans for the Patch?"

Diana's mouth tightened. "Ah, the infamous Riverview Exchange. Yes, it was the main topic at last month's town council meeting. I argued for preserving at least part of the parcel as a proper park, but I was outvoted. Five to one."

"I'm sorry."

"Don't be. I'm used to being the lone voice of opposition." Diana sipped her coffee. "Besides, this fight's only getting started. Despite their unified public front there are some tensions between the other council members."

"How do you know that?"

Diana chuckled. "Apparently people think having low vision means I can't hear, either. Folks seem to forget I'm in the room and say the most revealing things in front of me."

"How did you end up on the town council, anyway?" Rory asked. "I thought you'd stepped away from public service after ...."

"After I was forced into early retirement?" Diana

completed the thought without bitterness. "I tried, believe me. Had every intention of raising orchids and reading mystery novels. That lasted about three months before the boredom nearly killed me. I told the council they could give me a seat or defend my unlawful termination in court." She grinned. "Besides, someone needs to keep an eye on Ron."

The town council had used Diana's disability as an excuse to push her out and install her ex-husband, Ron, as chief. By all accounts, Diana had been a driven, fair, and incorruptible police chief. By all accounts, her ex-husband was none of these.

Rory glanced at her watch. "I should take this to go. I've got calls to make about the exhibition."

Diana tilted her head. "Which one? You have two, after all."

"The Pittsburgh show's been canceled. Creative differences with the gallery owner. I'm surprised you haven't already heard. Julie's been spreading the news."

"I take anything that woman says with an entire pillar of salt."

Rory choked back a laugh.

Diana reached across the table and squeezed her hand. "I'm sorry about your setback, though. Your work is important to this town, to the whole region. Don't let anyone diminish that."

Rory was surprised to find herself blinking back grateful tears as she headed outside.

She crossed the street and settled on a bench in a small green space on the square—another of Julie's improvements. Rory had to admit this one was genuinely beneficial. The wedge of grass featured native plantings, a Little Free Library, and comfortable seating. She sipped her drink and unfolded the newspaper to read the article.

The piece was mostly accurate, describing the *Vanishing Coal Country* exhibition as "a visual exploration of economic and cultural shifts along the Great Allegheny Passage." It quoted Professor Evan Jeffries at length about the historical significance of documenting these changes. The only problem was the article ended by promoting *Push/Pull* at the Hot Metal Gallery, a show that wouldn't happen. At least it didn't promise nude selfies, she comforted herself with a wry laugh.

Her phone buzzed persistently in her pocket, vibrating against her thigh. No wonder Tripp was blowing up her phone. His gallery was probably fielding inquiries about her now-canceled show. Lack of interest, huh?

She'd have to deal with him at some point, though. She might as well get it over with. But when she pulled out her phone, it wasn't Tripp's name flashing on the screen. It was Lucas's. Hot anger flared in her belly. Lucas may be Tripp's closest friend, but he had no right to insert himself into her career, not now. Not after everything.

They'd met when she was nineteen and he was thirty-two, a rising star in fashion photography. He'd shot her for *Vogue*, then asked her to dinner. The power imbalance should have been a red flag, but she'd been young, awestruck, and flattered by the attention.

For a while, they'd been good together. Lucas introduced her to photography, encouraged her interest in being behind the camera instead of in front of it. He bought her first serious camera—a Canon 5D Mark III—as a gift for her twenty-first birthday. It was the first time anyone had treated her as anything other than a beautiful face.

As she delved into photography and developed her own style, her work began to attract attention. And that's when everything changed. Lucas's encouragement turned to disparagement. He deemed her compositions amateur; her use of light and shadow, predictable; and her choices of subject, pedestrian. Around the same time, he began to critique her appearance, pointing out imaginary flaws, asking if she'd put on weight, had slept poorly, really intended to wear *that*.

The final straw was the tantrum he threw on the set of her first paid shoot. A niche Brooklyn arts magazine had invited her to do a photojournalistic piece on public art. She arranged a shoot in the Pratt Institute's Sculpture Park and called in some favors from fellow models to pose for a pittance. Her excitement was through the roof. But Lucas, who'd been in a foul mood for days, showed up uninvited and criticized everything from the lighting to the models to her aperture speed—publicly and at full volume.

She'd had campus security remove him and finished the shoot. Then she gave him time to cool off before going home to the apartment they shared. Instead of using the time to reflect, he got plastered. When she confronted him about his behavior, he grabbed her camera and hurled it at the wall behind her. She moved out the same night.

In the six years since, she'd earned a BFA in

photography and built her career focusing on documentary photography. She had a hard-won reputation for being a deliberate, thoughtful photographer with a talent for evoking emotion. She knew her work would speak to a larger audience—if she could only find one.

Calling in a favor to get the show at Hot Metal had felt like swallowing broken glass, but she'd believed it was worth it. It wasn't. Not if Lucas had really told Tripp to try to coerce her into including nude photos in the show. Nudes. Like some hormonal fourteen-year-old.

On second thought, she decided, Tripp could deal with the fallout without her. She deleted her messages without reading them and blocked both Tripp's and Lucas's numbers. She didn't need Lucas's connections or Tripp's gallery. She had her own contacts.

She scrolled through her phone and found Professor Jeffries' number. The director of the Western Trail History Center had been an early champion of her work, featuring it in a small group exhibition last year. And now he was showcasing her visual history of the miners who lived in the company town in *Vanishing Coal Country*. Evan had connections at most of the region's cultural institutions. If anyone could help her find a new home for *Push/Pull* on short notice, he could.

The call connected on the third ring.

"Rory! Are your ears burning? The volunteers are all buzzing about the article in the *Herald*. We're expecting a crowd today."

The professor's obvious delight made her smile

despite her current mess. "That's great to hear. I'm actually calling to see if you could brainstorm a solution to a problem with me."

"I'd love to. The center doesn't open to the public until noon. Can you swing by this morning?"

"I'm on my way."

10

———————

The Western Falls History Center, outside Union Hill

Evan Jeffries, Ph.D., sat on a curved bench in the small, empty lobby. The history center had closed almost an hour ago, and the last volunteers had left, flipping the sign on the door to 'closed.' Evan stood and walked through the exhibit space, turning off lights as he went. He paused in front of the replica company home set up in the biggest of the four rooms. Incredibly, the small wooden structure that had housed an entire family fit within the room.

He imagined what life must have been like for the children who'd grown up in the cramped quarters. Had they played jacks on the rough-hewn floors? Gathered around the pot-bellied stove for warmth? Chased their siblings through the narrow hallways?

Then he reminded himself that these long-ago children hadn't experienced much of a childhood at all. Many of the boys left school and joined their fathers in the mines when they were as young as eight or nine—working six days a week as breaker boys, separating out slate and other impurities from the anthracite. And the girls, not permitted to work in the mines, helped their mothers try to stretch their pennies at the overpriced company store, as well as with the washing and cooking.

No, it wasn't a pretty past. Not one to cast a nostalgic glow over. But it was the history of this region, and it was being erased.

It *had* been being erased, but no longer. Thanks to Aurora Westin. The photos and the oral histories she gathered from the surviving miners would preserve their stories and the story of the region for future generations.

He walked back through the lobby, let himself out, and locked the door behind him. He was grateful to Rory and genuinely wanted to help her get eyeballs on her new exhibition. He hoped that the plan they'd cooked up earlier in the morning would do just that.

As he started the short walk to his cottage situated off the trail before it reached Union Hill, he thought back over their conversation.

She'd begun by explaining that the show in Pittsburgh had been abruptly canceled. "Over creative differences," she'd said. But the tightness around her mouth and the set of her slim shoulders suggested the differences had perhaps been more personal than artistic.

Evan didn't pry. The reason was immaterial—whatever had precipitated it, the exhibit had been summarily canceled on short notice. And Rory was scrambling to find a new location to host the installation. Despite his reserve, after a moment, the ugly truth behind the cancellation spilled out of her.

He could have suggested the art school at the college where he taught. Or another history center or museum in the region. Even a church fellowship hall or a library. He knew people. He had colleagues and friends who worked at all these places and more. One of them, he imagined, would have been happy to provide Rory with a space.

But he didn't mention any of them. It was clear to Evan that she needed more than a location—she needed an event. He'd crossed his legs at the ankles and rocked back in his chair. It was his thinking pose. She'd waited patiently until he sprang forward again.

"We need to borrow a page from protest art," he declared.

"Protest art? It's not really a protest. Yes, it's social commentary, but—"

"—Fine then, activist art," he amended, warming to the subject. "From what you've told me about *Push/Pull* it goes beyond what the work you've done in *Vanishing Coal Country*. You've not only recorded the stories you're telling, you're not only asking the viewer to feel something, to consider a point of view, you're taking a stance. Aren't you?"

He watched her consider the question. Finally, slowly, she said, "I suppose I am. I'm not simply presenting the situation. I'm, well, I'm making a judgment."

She looked slightly queasy at this realization. He hurried to assure her, "It's perfectly acceptable to stake out a position, Rory."

"I guess. But I'm not one of the people being displaced. I don't want to be predatory or to use them in some way." She struggled to articulate her concern.

"Ah, but haven't you been displaced? Otherwise, you'd be hanging your photos in the Hot Metal gallery."

Once she'd seen the righteousness of her position, the idea to make a splash through a guerrilla art installation had seemed natural, almost inevitable. And he was more than happy to help her make it a reality.

He reached his front door, slightly winded from his brisk pace, and turned the key in the lock. He stepped inside, switched on the lamp, and stooped to pet Kathleen Guinan. The tuxedo cat wound herself around Evan's ankle, rubbing her head on Evan's shin and purring loudly.

"Ready for dinner?" he asked the cat, who responded by running to the pantry where her kibble was stored.

After feeding Kathleen Guinan and then himself, Evan went to bed early with a snifter of brandy and a well-worn copy of *Homelessness in America: A Forced March to Nowhere*. Tomorrow would be a long and busy day. He'd be wise to get a good night's sleep.

11

GAP Mile 104.7, Clarksville, PA

As Bodhi reached the Clarksville trailhead, a burly, barrel-chested man rose from a metal bench and took a pull from a vape pen. His beard was gray and neatly trimmed, and his substantial belly strained against a t-shirt featuring an anthropomorphic hamburger with an improbably wide grin.

"You Doctor King?" the man called when Bodhi was still twenty paces away.

"Bodhi's fine," he replied, closing the distance between them. His eyes flicked to the hamburger logo and the words "Billy's Burgers" emblazoned beneath it. "I'm guessing you're Billy."

The man's smile was even wider than that of the cartoon hamburger on his shirt. "I go by Will, but Billy's Burgers has a better ring to it, marketing-wise. Alliteration." He extended a beefy hand, which Bodhi shook. "Aunt Dot called ahead. She told me to fix you a meatless meal and put you up for the night."

"That sounds like Dot." Bodhi laughed as he shifted his pack slightly to relieve the pressure on his shoulders.

"She's not really my aunt, but don't tell her I said that." Will jerked his thumb toward a red sedan parked behind him. "Figured I'd save you the extra mile of walking into town. Hope that's okay."

"I appreciate it."

As Will drove, Bodhi lowered the passenger window and studied the town rolling by. In contrast to Clayton Falls' picture-perfect town square, Clarksville appeared to have missed the revitalization train entirely. They passed one boarded-up storefront after another, their faded signs nothing more than obituaries for long-dead establishment. Only a handful of businesses showed signs of life: a grocery store; a vape shop; and a tavern called The Last Stop, its neon beer signs blinking in the late afternoon sun.

"Not much to see," Will commented, seeming to read Bodhi's thoughts. "Used to be different. Had three factories running at once—glass, steel fabrication, and railroad parts. Last one closed in '08." He navigated around a pothole large enough to swallow the sedan's front tire. "The trail brings through tons of cyclists and hikers like you, but they don't stop here. Why would they when they could stay someplace like Clinton Falls or Union Hill?"

"Places with more amenities," Bodhi observed.

Will grunted his agreement. "The town's tried to get grants, attract investors, lure developers with tax breaks. Nobody bites." He turned down a narrow road that led away from the main strip. "My place is just up ahead, on the lake."

Lake was a generous description for the small, murky body of water that appeared as they reached the outskirts of town. A handful of trailer homes dotted its perimeter, interspersed with patches of scrubby woods. As they crested a rise, a squat building came into view. A large sign with the same cartoon hamburger from Will's shirt identified it as Billy's Burgers.

Will pulled into the gravel lot beside the building. "Home sweet home," he said, gesturing toward a small, tan-colored ranch house set back about fifty yards from the burger stand.

Bodhi eyed the burger place. "Do you get much business on the lake?"

"Well, the burger stand used to be a bait shop. I worked there in high school. After a stint in the Army, I came back and bought it and the house back there and opened Billy's Burgers. Nobody fishes in the lake. I mean look at it. But folks have to eat."

They walked past the burger joint and up the gravel drive to the house. Will unlocked the door and ushered Bodhi into a modest living room. The space was tidy but dated, with a plaid sofa, a recliner, and a TV that looked to be at least fifteen years old.

Will gestured to the hallway that ran to the left. "You can drop your bag in the bedroom back there. Just ignore all the stuffed animals. It was my daughter's room. She moved to Philly for college, but her teddy bears and bunny rabbits still call this place home."

It took a moment for Bodhi to realize Will wasn't

offering to help him find a hotel room—he was opening his home to a stranger.

When he caught on, he began to protest. "I don't want to impose. I'm sure I can find someplace—"

"Aunt Dot would have my hide if I let you stay anywhere else," Will interrupted with a good-natured firmness that made it clear he considered the issue settled. "Besides, it's just me here since Jessie moved out. Plenty of room. Not only that, I'm pretty sure the motel in town has bedbugs."

"In that case, I'm very grateful."

Will shrugs off his thanks. "No worries. You can wash up if you want. Bathroom's down the hall. I need to open the stand in twenty. Dinner rush'll start soon."

Bodhi thanked him and took the opportunity to shower and change into clean clothes. When he emerged, refreshed, Will was already gone. Through the living room window, Bodhi saw exterior lights illuminating the burger stand, and a pair of cars pulling into the lot.

Following the path to the metal building, Bodhi found Will working alone, flipping burgers on a flat-top grill with one hand while dropping fresh-cut potatoes into a fryer with the other.

"Need a hand?" Bodhi offered, observing the growing line of customers at the window.

Will glanced up, relief evident in his expression. "You know your way around a kitchen?"

"I've worked in a few."

"Then grab that apron and man the fryer. I never turn down help during the rush."

Bodhi tied the faded black apron around his waist and took up position at the fryer station. For the next two hours, they worked in seamless choreography. Will handled the grill and orders, Bodhi managed the fryer and assembled the completed meals.

As he passed meals through the service window, Bodhi caught snippets of the customers' conversations. There was a lot of discussion about a long-delayed road repair, some speculation about a potential buyer for the abandoned glass factory, and hushed gossip about someone's daughter who'd moved back from Columbus with a mysterious boyfriend.

"Hear about that photographer lady?" one man asked his companion as Bodhi handed them their onion rings. "The one taking pictures of all the old buildings before they get torn down?"

She nodded. "Yeah, my sister works in the bakery up in Union Hill. She says that photographer used to be a model. Like, famous. Victoria's Secret or something."

"No kidding? What's she doing around here?"

The woman shrugged. "Taking pictures of dying towns, I guess. They say she's documenting how the trail's changing everything."

"She oughta come here if she wants to see a dead town," the guy said as they walked away from the window.

After the rush subsided, Will prepared a burger for himself and a plate of fries with a side of sautéed vegetables for Bodhi.

"Not much of a vegan meal," he apologized as he set the food in front of Bodhi. "But the fries are just potatoes and vegetable oil, and the veggies are just ... well, vegetables."

"It's great," Bodhi assured him. "Thank you."

They ate at a picnic table Will had set up behind the stand. Bodhi watched as the sky transitioned from blue to deep purple. The lake reflected the sunset's colors, temporarily transforming its muddy surface into something beautiful.

"My daughter's a vegetarian," Will said between bites of his burger. "Not fully vegan, but still. When she comes home to visit, I try to have better options for her." He gestured with a fry. "She's always sending me recipes to try. Some of them aren't half bad. If I'd have known you were coming, I'd have had more to offer you."

"This is perfect. How long has she been away?"

"Two years now. Full scholarship to Penn." Pride warmed Will's voice. "Jessie's one heck of smart kid. Getting an engineering degree. Says she's going to come back and help revitalize places like Clarksville, but ...." He trailed off and focused on his burger.

"But you're not sure she will," Bodhi finished.

Will swallowed a bite. "I'm not sure she *should*. This place can't compete with the opportunities in Philadelphia or Pittsburgh. I won't blame her if she stays away. Most young folks do."

They finished their meal. While Will prepped for the next day, Bodhi washed and dried the dishes. As Will turned out the lights and rolled down the metal door, a car sped into the lot, spraying gravel in its wake.

They turned to see two men stepping out of a silver sports car, its engine still running. Bodhi couldn't see their faces because they were backlit by the car's bright LED headlights.

"Sorry, we're closed," Will called, shielding his eyes.

"We're famished. If you reopen, we'll make it worth your while," the driver countered.

From his tone, Bodhi guessed he was no stranger to solving his problems with money.

"Sorry," Will repeated flatly.

"Come on, pal," the second man entreated.

Bodhi strained to make out any details about the pair. He thought they might be wearing hiking or biking clothes despite arriving in a car. He hoped they weren't planning to stay at the bedbug motel before starting on the trail.

"You should head about twenty miles west. You'll hit a town called Clayton Falls. They have restaurants that stay open late."

"That's backtracking," the driver protested. "We're hiking toward Cumberland."

"Looks to me like you're driving." Will turned his back, ending the conversation, and started up the driveway.

After a moment, Bodhi followed him. Behind him, the car doors slammed, the engine roared back to life, and the pair departed with a squeal of tires.

Will and Bodhi settled on Will's back porch with cold drinks from his kitchen—a craft beer for Will, a glass of lemonade for Bodhi. The night was cool but not uncomfortable, filled with the gentle chorus of frogs from the lake and the distant hoot of an owl.

Will took a long pull from his beer and then resumed their conversation about young people leaving the town as if it had never been paused. "When they first converted the old rail line to a trail, folks around here thought it would be our salvation. Tourism dollars, new businesses catering to cyclists and hikers. Some towns saw that happen. This one, not so much."

"What do you think accounts for the difference?"

"Location, partly. Scenery. Existing infrastructure." Will gestured with his bottle. "But I think it's mostly about investment. Money flows toward money, right? Towns like Union Hill had people with capital come in, buy up property, and create that quaint trail town vibe that attracts the wealthy outdoors crowd. Why break ground here and start from scratch when you could go someplace already established?"

"You just need one investor willing to take a leap of faith."

Will shook his head. "Who, some rich prick like those guys who wanted me to reopen the shack? I'll pass."

"No, not outsiders. Surely there's a community organization that could provide seed money or a grant."

"That's a double-edge sword. Look at Clayton Falls. Like I said, they got an economic development grant from the county tourism board and started fixing up the square. But the grant wasn't renewed, and now despite that little pocket of prosperity, the rest of town is in worse shape than it was in the first place. All they managed to do was create the haves and the have nots."

Bodhi thought of Joey, out of options and drowning his pain, and nodded. "I get it."

Will mused, "It's too late for us. Clarksville's been

left behind. The cyclists and hikers only stop here for water, maybe a quick bite, and then they're on their way to the nicer towns. I don't blame them. I'd probably do the same in their shoes."

He drained his beer bottle, then stretched and yawned. "Anyway, I should turn in. Early start tomorrow."

Bodhi followed him inside. He brushed his teeth, stretched his tired body, and climbed into the twin bed in Jessie's room, surrounded by foxes, floppy-eared rabbits, and teddy bears of all sizes. Within minutes, the faint sound of the lake waters lapping against the shore lulled him to sleep.

12

———

Union Hill

When Rory returned to her studio, her conversation with Professor Jeffries was still buzzing in her mind. Evan had been encouraging but pragmatic: without the backing of an established gallery like Hot Metal, she needed to create something different, something that would generate its own attention.

"Art that demands to be seen often creates its own gallery," Evan had said thoughtfully. "Sometimes the most impactful exhibitions happen outside traditional spaces."

An idea had taken root immediately. If Tripp wouldn't show her work because she refused to commodify her body, she'd create her own exhibition —one that couldn't be canceled or compromised. She honestly wasn't sure whether she'd suggested it first or if Evan had. Either way, she knew it was the right next move. In fact, it was the only next move.

She dropped her bag on the floor and headed straight for her workstation. Her hands sped over her keyboard in a blur as she opened her editing software and began selecting images from yesterday's session with Lydia. The demolition photos were raw and visceral—the hydraulic arm of the excavator tearing through generations of memories, Lydia's face a study in dignified rage, Julie Mason surveying the destruction from behind a pair of designer sunglasses.

She selected the most powerful images and began making adjustments, losing herself in the familiar rhythm of her work. The world beyond her screen fell away as she focused on contrast, shadows, and highlights to bring out the emotional truth of each frame.

Hours later, she stood and stretched. As she stood in front of her large-format printer and watched it spit out the final print in the series, she noted with surprise that it was seven in the evening and that she'd worked through both lunch and dinner.

She gathered the eight photographs from the printer and carefully arranged them on her worktable, then stepped back to take in the narrative they created. Almost right. She switched two images and smiled. Perfect. She was exhilarated and tired all at once.

She reached for her phone and dialed Lydia's number.

"Hello?"

"Lydia, it's Rory Westin. I've been working with the photographs from yesterday, and I want to ask your permission to use them. To share them publicly." She suddenly felt uncertain about her idea.

There was a long silence on the line, which did nothing to bolster her flagging confidence.

Then Lydia said, "Why?"

"Because what happened to you matters. Because people should see it. Not just as some abstract concept of progress or economic development, but as something real that happens to real people. They tore down your home, but we don't have to let them erase your story."

Another pause, then a soft sigh. "You know, when you showed up yesterday with your fancy camera looking the way you do, I thought there was no way you could understand."

Rory winced. "I get it."

Lydia went on, "Then I saw how you looked at things. How you waited for the right moment. You weren't just taking pictures. You were bearing witness. So, go ahead. Use them. Show everyone what Julie Mason and her friends on the town council did."

Relief washed over Rory. "Thank you. I'll send digital copies to your daughter's email address, and I promise to send prints once they're ready."

"I can't wait to see them." Lydia hesitated, before adding, "My granddaughter has heard of you. She says your photographs make people feel things they'd rather ignore. Seems to me that's pretty important."

After Rory ended the call, she sent the digital files to Lydia's daughter with a brief note. Then she turned to the task at hand. The prints for *Push/Pull* leaned against the wall of her studio, waiting to be matted and framed before she took them to Pittsburgh to be hung. Now they had a different destiny.

She worked methodically, selecting the most powerful images from *Push/Pull* and the new series featuring Lydia. Using a thin wire and clips, she created a makeshift hanging system across her living room. Then, she pressed the button on her wall to lower the seldom-used outdoor privacy screen across the French doors leading to her balcony. Finally, she hung the large-format photographs from the clips, spacing them across her living space so they would be clearly visible from the courtyard below when the time was right.

Framed by open French doors, the images would create a dramatic visual statement that would be impossible to ignore for anyone passing by. It wasn't a gallery show, but in some ways, it was better. More immediate, more democratic, more defiant.

Spent, she headed to her kitchen to make a quick meal. The digital clock on her microwave told her three more hours had passed and it was now nearly eleven p.m. So she scratched the idea of dinner, settling for a glass of prosecco and a handful of nuts, both consumed leaning against the kitchen counter. Beatrice would have been appalled.

Rory was tired and wired. She needed to relax, wind down so she could get a decent night's sleep. She refilled her glass and headed into her spa-like bathroom. She shed her clothes and pressed the button on the wall outside her glass shower enclosure to activate the steam generator. Then she stepped into the shower and stretched out on the built-in bench to sip her drink and let the booze and the steamy heat melt away the tension, conflict, and worry of her day.

13

———————

GAP Mile 92.3, Between Clarksville and Union Hill

After a breakfast of toast topped with peanut butter and Will's homemade berry preserves, Bodhi consulted his trail guide and map to prepare for his day's walk.

"Where to today?" Will asked.

"Union Hill. But I want to stop at the history center outside town before it closes."

Will leaned over the map. "You'll have to hustle. That place closes at four."

"You've been?"

Will nodded. "Couple times. Dot and my mom are big history nerds. Sometimes they drag me along. It's worth seeing. I hear they have a new exhibit about the coal town."

"Do you want to join me?"

"Wish I could, but I only close for a few hours between the lunch rush and dinner."

"That's my cue." Bodhi shouldered his pack. "Thanks again for letting me stay here. It was kind of you."

Will brushed off his gratitude. "Any friend of Aunt Dot's is welcome here. Besides, you saved my bacon, er, tofu, during the dinner rush." He handed Bodhi a small paper bag. "Some apples and homemade granola for the trail. Union Hill's a good hike from here."

They stepped out onto the porch and walked as far as the burger stand together.

"You sure you don't want a lift to the trailhead?"

"Positive." He'd kept the man from his work long enough.

"Okay, then just follow the road until you get to the vape shop. You can cut across the park to meet up with the trailhead instead of staying on the road. It'll save you some time."

"Appreciate it."

"Take care," Will said.

They shook hands, then Bodhi set off on the path that wound around the far side of the lake.

As he followed the curve of the path, he saw Will rolling up the burger stand's metal door to start his day's work. He climbed the hill, and Will shrank to a pinprick in the distance.

Bodhi hugged the road's narrow shoulder as it wound toward town. Traffic was light, but most of the drivers zipping by him seemed to take the posted speed limit as a gentle suggestion. When he reached the vape shop and saw the sign for the

Clarksville Community Park, he let out a soft, relieved sigh.

He waited for a break in the traffic to cross over to the park entrance. As he was about to step into the street, a silver sports car sped toward him, coming from the direction of Clayton Falls. He jumped back.

A second later, the car screeched to an abrupt stop as a school bus headed toward Clayton Falls stopped and extended its stop-sign arm. As the driver opened the door to pick up a gaggle of middle schoolers, Bodhi studied the occupants of the car—identified by its badge as a Jaguar. Two men, both clad in fleece jackets, sat, staring straight ahead, not speaking as they waited for the bus driver to close the door and pull in the stop sign.

He wondered idly if this was the same car and the same men who'd shown up at Billy's Burgers after Will had closed up last night. He turned to take a closer look at the pair, but just then the bus pulled away, and the Jaguar shot forward and raced away, the loud purr of the engine fading as the car disappeared from view.

He crossed the street, walked past a basketball court that featured a pair baskets with ripped and dangling nets, one backboard missing its glass. Then he cut through the empty playground and found the footpath that led to the GAP trail.

When he reached a fenced-in private yard, he thought he'd strayed from his course until he read the small wooden sign mounted near the gate: Hikers and bikers, please be sure to close and latch both gates behind you. Safe travels.

He did as instructed, sending his gratitude to the

property owners who saw fit to share their access to the GAP freely.

On the other side, the trail widened. Twenty yards later, he spotted the marker that meant he was back on the GAP. The path unspooled at his feet, pulling him forward toward Union Hill.

14

———

Union Hill

R ory woke fuzzy-headed and dry-mouthed. Dehydrated, no doubt, from her poor choices the night before. She hauled herself out of bed and headed to the kitchen on shaky legs for a glass of water. She remembered the ad hoc art installation in her living room before she reached the hallway.

She detoured to her studio to grab her camera and ran to the living room to raise the privacy screen and fling open her French doors. Then, she raced down to the cobblestone courtyard barefoot and still wearing her pajamas. She clambered up to the rooftop deck outside the tapas restaurant and wine bar to peer into her own living room at the narrative the prints told: A story of coal miners, mothers, teenagers, widows, and business owners losing their spaces juxtaposed with developers, tourists, business owners, and newcomers taking their places. In a small irony, the exhibit included one self-portrait—Rory's reflection in the glass of the ancient grains bakery.

She lifted her viewfinder to her eye and focused on the display, firing off several shots. Then she ran back down to the courtyard and sprinted up the stairs to her apartment. Out of breath, she grabbed her laptop and typed a statement to accompany the images:

Push/Pull: An Exhibition of Displacement

We preserve what we value. We discard what we don't.

All along the Great Allegheny Passage, communities are being transformed. Some are being revitalized, pulling in new visitors, new residents, new businesses. Others are being left behind, withering away from neglect and lack of opportunity. And still others are being demolished, hollowed out from within as longtime residents are pushed aside to make way for a new vision of prosperity.

Portions of this now-expanded installation were originally meant to be exhibited in Pittsburgh's Hot Metal Art Gallery. That showing has been canceled due to creative differences. I never wanted to insert myself into this narrative, but now I realize I'm in it whether I like it or not.

So I'm taking this exhibition out of the exclusive gallery space and putting it where it belongs—in plain sight, in the communities being affected, visible to everyone regardless of whether they can afford gallery admission or feel comfortable in curated art spaces.

These photographs are only the beginning. Over the coming days, I'll be documenting more sites along the trail where people and their stories are being erased in the name of progress. These new visual histories will be posted on my website and social media pages in real time.

To see the truth, we cannot look away.
—Aurora Westin

She forwarded several of the photos from her camera to her laptop and attached the best images of the window installation, as well as copies of each of the individuals photo hanging from her ceiling, and broadcast the post across her social media channels. Then she forwarded it to her small newsletter list; Evan Jeffries; the *Herald* reporter who'd interviewed her; and all her professional contacts. After a moment's hesitation, she decided not to delete Tripp and Lucas's addresses from the email. Let them see what they'd tried to suppress.

Responses began flooding in immediately. But she didn't pause to savor the moment. She needed to execute the rest of her plan to continue to document —and to experience, however briefly—displacement.

She would travel light, carrying only her camera and essentials. She grabbed her weatherproof messenger bag and began packing. She tossed her Nikon D850 with two lenses, extra batteries, memory cards, a small notebook, protein bars, a water bottle, a light rain jacket, a change of clothes, and basic toiletries into the bag. She almost left her phone on the charger as a statement, but she needed a way to post images as she traveled. So she grabbed it and added it to the bag along with a travel charger.

She took her wallet from her desk drawer and removed her driver's license and three twenties, which she slipped into the messenger bag's zippered pocket. Then she returned the wallet with the rest of her cash and all her credit cards to the drawer. To document displacement authentically, she needed to know how it felt to leave everything behind, even if only temporarily. The gesture felt theatrical, but she committed to it anyway.

She did a quick sweep of the apartment, trying to shake the feeling that she was forgetting something important. The exhibition was hanging. The statement was circulating. Her camera was packed. She had water and food. What else did she need?

The murmur of voices drifted up from the courtyard. She peered down and saw a small crowd forming, their necks craned as they gazed up at her window in the early-morning light. The rooftop deck across the square was filling with people trying to get a better view.

It was time to go. If she waited any longer, her plan to slip away unnoticed would be ruined.

She hoisted her bicycle over her shoulder and carried it down the back stairs, emerging into the alley behind Railroad Way. She mounted the seat and pedaled quickly down the hill, staying on side streets until she reached the trail access point at the other end of town, well away from the growing commotion around her impromptu exhibition.

The Great Allegheny Passage stretched out ahead of her like a ribbon, or maybe a promise.

15

Sadie slammed the stockroom door and dropped a pile of vests on the counter. Aaron's back was to her, but she clocked the tension in his shoulders. She tried to hide her irritation, but she could tell by the way his eyes flicked toward her every time she cut open a box of merchandise with a little too much force or the way he stiffened when she banged the cash register closed too loudly that he knew she was pissed.

The fact that he registered her annoyance made her even more frustrated. She had every right to be mad. Didn't she? Her anger abated when she answered her own rhetorical question: sure, but she was really mad at herself, not him.

Her relationship with Aaron was far from healthy. If she were being honest, it bordered on toxic. Every time they broke up, she promised herself this time it was for good. And every time, she took him back. Her friends pressed her for an explanation, but she couldn't explain it to them because she didn't understand it herself. Well, she *sort of* understood it.

He made her laugh. He made her feel light and carefree and, she had to admit, sexy.

The youngest store manager in Outdoor Adventure Co-op history and on a clear upward trajectory, Sadie was, as a rule, the opposite of light and carefree. She was ambitious and focused and, just maybe, a tiny bit humorless. Aaron, in contrast, was friendly and easygoing but, at best, a mediocre hourly employee. And in her heart, she knew that even that assessment was too generous. Despite the fact that they'd been dating, sleeping together, and/or living together for most of his employment, he'd been on probation more than once. Inevitably, she was going to have to fire him someday. Still, she kept taking him back.

Their living arrangement didn't help. During their breaks or breakups or whatever you wanted to call them, she would remind herself to be strong, to treat him just as a roommate and nothing more. Yet inevitably he'd show up at her bedroom door with a couple of craft IPAs and a pizza, suggesting a movie, and then the next thing she knew they'd be in a tangle of sheets.

None of this was in her plan. The plan was literal, not metaphorical. Sadie had mapped it out in a spreadsheet during her first year of college. She hadn't come to Union Hill for some on-again off-again relationship with a stoner. She'd graduated *summa cum laude* with a business degree and a plan to launch her own B corporation someday, an outdoor company committed to the public benefit. Working for OAC was a step in that plan.

And then she'd met Aaron. Despite his lack of ambition—or maybe because of it—he made her stomach do somersaults. So while the local mean girls thought she was jealous of Rory, they were wrong. She was disappointed in herself for her weakness. Ashamed of the way she took Aaron back so easily. All it took was a grin and a suggestion, and she brought him into her bed again—even though he was still, after all this time, mooning over Rory Westin. It was humiliating.

The display yesterday where he trotted over to her like a golden retriever with the newspaper had turned Sadie's stomach. He'd been so eager for a pat on the head that she was surprised he hadn't carried it in his mouth. She'd been embarrassed for him and for herself.

Yes, Rory was a talented photographer. Good for her. And she was beautiful—a knockout. Sadie had eyes, she couldn't deny the woman was stunning. And, she had to admit, Rory didn't capitalize on her looks. She dressed in jeans and t-shirts and wore almost no makeup. Some days, Sadie was sure she hadn't bothered to brush her hair. But despite all that, Aurora Westin was objectively gorgeous.

Sadie's eyes flicked over to the full-length mirror mounted on the wall outside the dressing rooms. Fit, strong, with dewy olive skin, clear green eyes, and glossy brown hair, she was the picture of health and natural beauty. Sure, she was no supermodel. But she was pretty, smart, and independent. Frankly, she was out of Aaron's league. But here they were. It was demoralizing.

As if he could hear her thoughts, Aaron turned to her. "Everything okay, babe?"

She mumbled a non-response. Eager to a fault to be liked, he left the pile of tents he was stickering with price tags and ambled over to her.

He dug his warm hands into her back and began massaging her tight shoulders. "You're so tense."

She felt herself melting under his touch even though she tried to resist. "I'm fine."

"You really aren't. Relax," he purred in her ear as he rubbed her knotted muscles with firm strokes.

She exhaled, allowing herself to soften into his touch.

Then, just as she was about to sigh with pleasure, he said, "Did you see the installation up the street?"

She stiffened.

His tone was light and casual, like he was trying to contain his excitement. He cared enough to do that, at least. But the question stung.

Of course, she'd seen it. How could she miss it? Everyone was buzzing about Rory's latest stunning achievement when she stopped in at Ember + Bean for her morning coffee. Her curiosity demanded she detour past Rory's building to check it out on her way to the store.

"What installation?" The lie flew out of her mouth on its own accord.

Before she could tease out the reason for her dishonesty, he was tripping over himself to tell her all about Rory's guerrilla art show. She tuned out and let his rush of words wash over her and roll away, as if they were water and she were the proverbial duck.

16

Rory pedaled fast, spurred on by a burst of excitement and anticipation as Union Hill receded into the distance. Despite her hard riding, she made slow progress. This was intentional. She made several stops, detouring off the trail to document the GAP's effects—intentional and otherwise—on the surrounding area.

Her stomach growled in protest. She ignored it and continued pedaling. She could eat and rest her jelly-like legs when she reached her first stopping point—a small cave set into a hillside about twelve miles west of Union Hill, eight miles east of Clarksville. The cave didn't appear on any trail maps and was accessible only by a barely visible path through dense underbrush. She'd stumbled across it during a bike ride soon after she moved to town. A crack of thunder announced a sudden storm while she was photographing the lichen on a felled tree alongside the trail. As the rain sheeted down, she spotted the cave above and scrabbled up the hillside to wait out the storm.

The deceptively narrow entrance opened up to a surprisingly spacious interior. She'd been content to shelter there and, when the rain stopped, was delighted to see that the sunlight hit the cave at an interesting angle. She'd taken a series of pictures before leaving and had returned several times since to photograph the way light filtered through the trees that shielded the mouth of the cave from sight. The cave was completely hidden from the trail.

By the time she reached the concealed turnoff, it was late afternoon. The sun was in the sky and the air was beginning to take on a chill. Leaning her bike against a tree, she followed the narrow path up the gentle slope until the mouth of the cave appeared through the foliage. Then it was a quick climb up the rocky hillside to the cave itself.

Inside, she settled on the smooth stone floor, unpacking her protein bars and water. The cave was cool but not yet cold. The slanting sunlight warmed her face and shoulders for now. And she had a warm jacket in her pack for later.

She nibbled on a chalky chocolate-flavored energy bar while she scrolled through the images on her camera's viewfinder, reviewing the photos she'd taken along the way: an abandoned gas station; the contrast between a row of sleek, expensive trail cycles lined up at an overlook awaiting their riders and a group of tired hospitality workers huddled under a bus shelter waiting for one of the handful of public buses still operating in the area; a wild, unmaintained section of the trail; and a half-collapsed barn in the process of being reclaimed by nature.

Rory transferred the images to her phone and made rudimentary edits. Then she typed out descriptions, checked them over for obvious typos, and uploaded the series to her website and shared them across her social media accounts. She hit send on the last photo and stood, slipping the phone into her pants pocket.

Her back twinged and her shoulders ached. She'd been hunched over her phone longer than she'd realized. She rolled her neck and shoulders and was mid-forward fold when she heard a familiar voice.

"Rory? I know you're up here somewhere. Your bike's at the trailhead."

She rolled up to standing, and a sudden stabbing abdominal pain nearly knocked her back down. She clung to the cave wall to brace herself as the pain in her midsection roared like a fire. Her heart raced and her breath came fast and shallow. Lightheaded and shaking, she tried to push herself up, but as nausea overcame her, she slid down the wall and doubled over, clutching her stomach.

Footsteps approached and a shadow fell across the cave's entrance. "Rory."

As she turned toward the sound of her name, she pitched forward, dizzy and sweating from the pain. Her palms connected with the rough cave floor and her forearms trembled from the effort of holding herself up. Her vision tunneled, and darkness seeped in from the periphery.

She managed to stand—for a moment. As she

swayed, she finally remembered what she'd forgotten to do. Then she was falling, and the hard cave floor rushed up to meet her.

PART III

.

Art is not what you see, but what you make others see.

— EDGAR DEGAS, FRENCH
IMPRESSIONIST PAINTER

What you see is what you see.

— FRANK STELLA, AMERICAN
MINIMALIST PAINTER

17

Bodhi spent more time than he'd intended at the history center, engrossed in the exhibit about the coal town. The photo essays were powerful, and the walk through the replica of the simple company home had made the miners' stories feel even more visceral and real. After watching the short film about the strikes that changed the industry in the early part of the twentieth century, he sat alone in the dark media room for a long while, absorbing what he'd learned. He sat there so long that a gray-haired man wearing round glasses and a cardigan sweater with leather-patched sleeves came in and apologetically told him that the center was closing.

When he left the history center, he walked at a brisk pace to make up some of the time. As a rule he didn't hurry, believing that wherever he happened to be was where he was meant to be. But he made an exception now because he wanted to reach Union Hill before nightfall.

As the sun dipped low and the shadows lengthened, he moved steadily—until he felt someone watching him. He stopped mid-stride and turned, his breath catching in his throat. Twenty feet ahead, a white-tailed deer stood motionless at the creek's edge where it ran parallel to the trail. The animal's stillness seemed contemplative. He watched until the doe blinked at him once, slowly, and lowered her head to drink.

He realized that he, too, was thirsty. He eased his pack off his shoulders and retrieved his water bottle, careful not to startle the deer. As he drank deeply, savoring the cool water, a sudden rustle broke the silence. The deer bounded into the understory, her white tail flashing between the trees as she disappeared from view.

As he tracked the trajectory of the doe plunging into the brush, his eye snagged on a flash of color behind the shrubs. Curious, he returned his water bottle to the side pocket of his pack and veered off the path to investigate. A shiny, candy apple red trail bike leaned against a tree trunk about thirty feet off the trail.

When he reached the precariously balanced bicycle, he scanned the area for its owner but saw no one. Looking down, he spotted signs of recent activity. The imprint of shoes in the dirt and a pile of broken twigs drew his attention to a barely visible path leading away from the trail. The path curved up a gentle slope. After a moment's consideration, he followed it.

The narrow path wound uphill through thickening undergrowth. Bodhi pushed aside low-hanging branches and stepped carefully over exposed roots. After about fifty yards, the vegetation thinned, revealing the dark mouth of a cave set into the hillside.

He paused at the entrance, waiting for his eyes to adjust to the dimmer light. His gaze swept over the cave floor and settled on a messenger bag lying on its side near the wall. Contents spilled from the open flap—protein bars, a phone charger, and what looked like camera equipment.

Then he saw it. Blood. A small, glistening pool with spatter radiating outward. His training kicked in automatically as he analyzed the pattern—the blood had been expelled with force, not from a minor cut or scrape.

He frowned and took a careful step forward, noting a partial shoe print in blood leading out of the cave. Several feet from the messenger bag, a single, blood-splattered cycling shoe lay on its side, its mate nowhere in sight. The shoe's tread didn't match the print on the cave's floor. Next to it, a small rectangle of colorful plastic caught his eye—a driver's license. He squatted to examine it without touching it.

Aurora Elin Westin. Her photo showed a classically beautiful young woman with striking white-blonde hair, intense blue eyes, and a warm smile.

He drew back in surprise. Rory? The photographer?

He made quick work of searching the rest of the cave but found no signs of Aurora herself or evidence of where she—or anyone who might have been with her—had gone.

Then he squatted beside the blood and snapped on a pair of blue nitrile gloves from the evidence kit he carried out of habit. He pressed one pointer finger into the puddle. When he drew his gloved finger back, it was covered with wet, barely tacky blood.

The blood—presumably Aurora's—had been spilled recently. In the past minutes, not hours.

He crashed through the trees, calling her name, making no effort to be stealthy. The more noise he made the better if she was injured and trapped somewhere nearby. But after twenty minutes of thrashing around in the woods, he'd seen no sign of her, and the only response to his calls had been an irritated bird scolding him.

He grabbed the items from the cave and returned to the trail, jogging at a steady clip. Union Hill couldn't be more than ten or twelve miles ahead. He needed to alert the authorities—the sooner, the better.

18

Union Hill

Diana Mercer tilted her head, using her peripheral vision to track the server weaving through the crowded rooftop deck of Vines & Vibes. The tapas and wine bar's prime corner table had an unobstructed view across the courtyard to Rory's apartment, where the impromptu exhibition continued to command the attention of the growing crowd. Diana, unable to appreciate the photographs from this distance, focused on the reactions of the rest of the onlookers.

"Another glass?" The server appeared at her elbow, gesturing toward her empty wine glass.

"One's my limit."

She gave her yellow-tinted glasses a soft tap as if reminding herself that she'd be wise to keep her intake moderate, no matter how tasty the reds on offer might be.

Julie Mason, seated to her right, lifted her own glass. "I'll take another tempranillo."

"And I'm fine as well," Evan Jeffries said from Diana's left. The history professor leaned forward, resting his leather-patched elbows on the table, his eyes fixed on Rory's photos across the courtyard. "Extraordinary work. The juxtaposition of light and shadow, the raw emotion in the subjects' faces—it demands a response."

Julie snorted softly. "You can say that again. Though I question her tactics."

Diana resisted the urge to roll her eyes. She'd known both Julie and Evan since high school, and some things never changed. Julie was the ambitious girl who escaped to the city, only to return to their tiny town years later as its self-proclaimed savior. Evan was the idealistic do-gooder who went off to college to soak up knowledge like a sponge and returned to his hometown to share it. She wondered idly what that made her.

As Evan huffed, Diana's musing was quickly supplanted by a silent hope that Julie and Evan wouldn't start one of their interminable debates. Evan, a democratic socialist and activist, and Julie, the consummate capitalist, were locked in an eternal battle as opponents over the proper direction of Union Hill's ongoing evolution.

While Evan was still winding up for his lecture, a stranger appeared on the deck. A lanky man with a tangle of dark, shoulder-length curls mounted the stairs and stood, scanning the crowd. He wore dusty hiking clothes and had a backpack settled on his shoulders. He carried a messenger bag in one hand and, incongruously, held a shoe in the other.

"Excuse me," the man said to nobody in particular in a deep, rich voice that carried across the now-hushed patio. "I'm looking for Diana Mercer."

As Evan and Julie turned to look at her in surprise, she lifted her hand. "Over here."

A path opened in the sea of bodies to allow the man to make his way to their table. He edged through the crowd with economical movements and stopped beside Diana's chair. She sensed, more than saw, tension in his posture.

"Ms. Mercer? I'm Bodhi King." He eased his pack off his shoulders and set it down beside the table but kept a tight grip on the messenger bag and the shoe. "I've just come from the police station."

What had Ron done now?

The question was still forming in her mind, when the man continued, "I went there to report a missing person, but the chief of police was disinclined to investigate."

She glanced at the bright digits on her oversized watch face. "Well, it's nearly time for his siesta," she deadpanned.

Julie snickered into her fresh glass of wine, and Evan shook his head.

Bodhi King gave her a patient, steady look.

Diana felt compelled to explain. "Chief Mercer is my ex-husband. He's never been accused of being proactive—or energetic." Then she frowned. "Although even Ron would ordinarily respond to a missing person's report. Especially one involving a tourist. Have you lost a hiking companion?"

"Not exactly. I found this." He rested the messenger bag on the table.

She leaned over it for a closer inspection, turning her head so she wasn't looking at it straight on. Julie leaned in, too. "That looks like Rory's bag."

"If Rory is Aurora Westin, I believe it is her bag. Her driver's license was on the ground beside it, along with some camera equipment."

"Where exactly did you find this, Mr. King?" Diana asked.

"Bodhi's fine. I'm hiking the trail from Pittsburgh. Today's mileage was Clarksville to here. I stopped at the Western Trail History Center this afternoon." He paused to nod at Evan, who snapped his fingers as if realizing that he recognized the hiker. "After I left there, I crossed a stream, approximately eight miles into my walk, and spotted an unattended bicycle off the side of the trail."

"A mountain bike?" Evan asked. "Bright red?"

Bodhi nodded. "Yes. I searched the immediate area for the owner. That's when I found this bag and its contents, along with this single cycling shoe, in a secluded cave."

"Just one shoe?" Diana murmured.

"Just the one," he confirmed. Then he went on, his voice resonant and somber, "There was also blood on the cave floor."

"Blood?" Julie echoed.

Evan sucked in a breath.

Diana drew her eyebrows together. "You reported all of this to the police chief?"

"Yes," Bodhi confirmed. "He informed me that the department didn't plan to waste resources on what he called Ms. Westin's publicity stunt."

She tightened her jaw and clamped her lips together to keep her inside thoughts inside.

"I pressed him and tried to explain that the situation could be serious. But he told me I was welcome to form a search party of volunteers if I was so concerned. Then he invited me to see myself out. As I was doing so, an officer named Sarah pulled me aside and suggested I find you. She said you might be here. She didn't explain why I should look for you."

Diana felt the weight of his gaze on her as if it were a physical thing. "Sarah sent you to me because before the current Chief Mercer was in charge, I led the police department for almost a decade."

She reached out and ran a light finger over the black messenger bag's strap. It was definitely Rory's bag. She rarely left her studio without it.

"Ah, that makes sense."

She peered at him. "Are you sure it was blood you saw? Could it have been something else?"

"I'm sure. I'm a forensic pathologist." He paused to let this information sink in. "It was blood, fresh blood. It was still wet, only just beginning to turn tacky to the touch."

"How fresh?" Evan wanted to know.

"Less than an hour old at that point."

"In a cave," Diana mused.

There were at least a half-dozen caves between here and Clarksville. She hoped the forensic pathologist could find it again. She also hoped they wouldn't be in need of his pathology skills.

"I might know the cave," Julie said quickly. "Rory photographed a cave last year for a tourism brochure I was putting together. She said most people walk right past it."

Diana pinched the bridge of her nose beneath her glasses, thinking. "You know where it is?"

Julie grimaced. "Well, not exactly."

Diana fell silent for a beat. Then she recovered her manners. "Bodhi, this is Julie Mason, she's a local developer."

"CEO of Mason Property and Development," Julie interjected, reaching for Bodhi's hand.

"Nice to meet you," he said before turning to Evan. "And we met at the history center, but we weren't formally introduced."

"Ah, yes. You're the gentleman I shooed out of the exhibit so I could close up. Evan Jeffries. Apologies for chasing you out."

Bodhi laughed. "No apology needed. I was there for a long time. The exhibit had a powerful effect on me."

Evan's face lit up with pride. Then he blinked at Bodhi from behind his glasses and gestured toward Rory's apartment across the way. "Are you aware of what's happening here?"

Bodhi shook his head. "No. I couldn't miss the crowd, but I don't know what all the excitement is about.

Diana gazed across the courtyard. Dusk had crept in and she could no longer make out the photographs in the dim light. Apparently, neither could anyone else.

Evan leaned forward, eager to explain. "Rory

created a guerrilla exhibition of her work after her gallery show in Pittsburgh was canceled. She's been documenting displacement along the Great Allegheny Passage—families and businesses pushed out by developers."

Diana didn't miss the sideways glance Evan gave Julie. Neither did Julie, who stiffened but said nothing.

"This afternoon, she unveiled the exhibit across the way in her apartment and then posted on social media that she planned to document more sites along the trail. That explains why she's out on the trail," Evan finished.

"It doesn't explain why she left her bike and camera behind," Diana said. "Or why she'd wander off wearing only one shoe."

"There's no way she'd leave her camera voluntarily," Julie agreed.

"It also doesn't explain the blood." Bodhi gave voice to what the rest of them wouldn't or couldn't.

After a beat, Diana said, "No. It doesn't."

"You didn't find her phone?" Evan asked.

"No phone," Bodhi confirmed.

Evan pulled out his cell phone and tapped a number eagerly, activated the speakerphone function, and placed the device on the table. They all leaned over it, waiting for it to ring. But the call went directly to voicemail without ringing.

"You've reached Rory. I rarely check my messages. Please text me instead."

Evan deflated as he jabbed the phone off. "It didn't even ring. It's either turned off or she doesn't have coverage."

"Or her battery's dead," Diana added. "Go ahead and text her anyway, Evan. It can't hurt."

As the professor thumbed out a text, Bodhi dropped his voice. "Did she have any history of mental illness? Depression? Suicidal ideation?"

"Not that I know of," Diana said.

"She wouldn't hurt herself," Julie said firmly. "That's not Rory."

"So if the police won't look for her, what do we do now?" Evan asked as he stowed his phone in his pocket.

"We look for her," Diana responded simply. "Do you think you could lead us back to her, Bodhi?" She asked the question to the table in general instead of attempting to make eye contact with the man in the fading light.

He turned toward her, positioning himself so that he was in her line of sight. Then he answered her question and asked one of his own. "I can find the cave again. If you don't mind my asking, how advanced is your AMD?" he asked.

His directness startled her. "What gave it away?"

"Small things. The way you track sounds rather than movement. How you oriented your head just now to use your peripheral vision as if you have a blind spot in the center of your vision. The yellow-tinted glasses to help with contrast."

"The dry form. Stable for now." She matched his matter-of-fact tone.

"Are you sure you're up for leading a search party?"

She pushed back her chair. "I'm up for joining it, but I won't be leading it. You will."

Before he could respond, Julie popped to her feet.

"I'm coming, too. I know this area better than most."

"Count me in as well," Evan added, buttoning his cardigan.

Bodhi surveyed the group. "It'll be dark by the time we get to the cave."

"We'll stop by the OAC store for gear. Headlamps, jackets, first-aid supplies, maybe some food," Julie suggested, signaling for the check.

Then their little group of four made their way through the thinning crowd and down the stairs. Bodhi offered Diana his arm, but she waved it away in favor of the railing. She counted the steps silently as they descended so she'd know when she hit the pavement.

By the time they reached the street, the sun had slipped below the horizon, and the retro street lamps and string lights blazed brightly. Diana realized they'd need more than headlamps if they wanted to start the search tonight.

As if he'd read her mind, Bodhi said, "We don't have the luxury of waiting until first light, unfortunately."

"I know," she said simply.

Rory was alone, bleeding in the woods. With each passing hour, the odds of finding her alive decreased.

19

———————

Bodhi matched Diana's pace as they followed Julie and Evan down the sidewalk toward the Outdoor Adventure Co-op. At the end of the block, the store's large display windows glowed invitingly, showcasing mannequins dressed for outdoor adventure alongside kayaks and camping gear.

He was acutely aware of two men who had been trailing them at a discreet distance since they'd left the tapas bar's deck. He leaned down, about to mention them to Diana. She placed her hand on his forearm and murmured, "I know."

Evan pulled open the large door and ushered the women and Bodhi inside. Rows of brightly colored technical jackets and sturdy hiking boots lined one wall. Kayaks, bicycles, and tents hung on the opposite wall. Camping gear, water bottles, and trail maps filled shelves that ran down the center of the store.

One of the two men caught the door before it closed, and the pair drifted into the shop behind Evan. They peeled off to the right and made their way through the aisles of camping equipment. They were dressed like through-hikers—moisture-wicking shirts, convertible pants, trail runners—but their gear was too new, too clean. One man still had a price tag tucked into the collar of his jacket. The other's shoes were immaculate and showed none of the scuffs and wear patterns of actual trail use.

"Diana!" A young man with an eager smile rushed over from behind the counter. His eyes landed immediately on the messenger bag she carried. "Is that—?" He stopped mid-sentence, his smile faltering.

"Yes, it's Rory's bag. Dr. King here found it on the trail along with her bicycle and some blood. We're organizing a search party."

Aaron's face paled. "Blood? Is she hurt? Where—?"

"We don't know yet," Diana cut in. "But we need gear. Headlamps, first-aid supplies, bright emergency lights if you have them. Maybe some food and water."

Aaron nodded vigorously. "Of course, anything." Then his eyes darted to the door set into the back wall behind the register. "I should get Sadie. She's in the stockroom. She knows the trail better than anyone."

As if summoned by her name, a woman with chestnut hair pulled into a practical ponytail emerged from the back. She took in the group with a quick, assessing glance.

"What's going on?" she asked, her green eyes narrowing when they landed on Aaron's anxious face.

Evan stepped forward. "Rory Westin is missing. We're putting together a search party."

Sadie's expression shifted from confusion to skepticism. "Missing? Since when? We just saw her yesterday. And then she unveiled her ... thing in her apartment this morning."

"Since this afternoon, at least," Bodhi said. He introduced himself and explained what he'd found.

Sadie listened with her arms folded across her chest. When he mentioned the blood, her eyes widened and she made a soft 'oh' sound. She checked the time. "I'll close up early and join you," she said, though Bodhi detected reluctance in her tone. "Aaron, get them whatever they need."

"Of course. And I'm coming, too."

"As if there was ever any doubt," she said dryly.

Bodhi raised an eyebrow at the exchange, and Julie leaned over to whisper, "It's a long story."

Sadie turned toward the pair of men who were pretending to examine headlamps. "The store's closing in ten minutes. Please make your selections now."

The taller of the two men stepped forward. "Actually, we couldn't help overhearing. We'd like to join the search."

Bodhi studied them more carefully. The taller one was around forty, with carefully tousled brown hair and the kind of tan that came from recreational rather than occupational sun exposure. His companion was slightly older, maybe fifty, with alert, appraising eyes, a pronounced widow's peak, and buffed and manicured fingernails. They looked strangely familiar. What was more, they sounded familiar.

Recognition hit him with a flash of insight. They were the men from outside Billy's Burgers. The men in the silver Jaguar.

"We're hiking the trail," the taller one continued. "We have equipment, experience. We want to help."

Diana cut a quick look to Bodhi. He shook his head almost imperceptibly. Ultimately, it was her decision. But he didn't trust them.

She cocked her head. "Thank you for the offer. I think we have all the help we need. This isn't going to be comfortable or fun. It's not the experience we advertise when we invite you to have an adventure in Union Hill," she said, softening the rejection with a smile.

A look passed between the men. After a beat, the older one spoke again. "I'm afraid we have to insist."

"You insist?" Diana's smile vanished.

For a moment, nobody spoke.

Bodhi hesitated, considering whether speaking up would violate the precept of right speech. While his beliefs forbade lying, they also prohibited divisive speech. And pointing out the men's dishonesty would not create harmony. He made up his mind that he couldn't let the lie pass unchallenged.

"But you're not really hiking the GAP, are you?"

"What do you mean?" the taller of the men demanded.

"You're traveling by car. A silver sports car."

The man dropped his gaze and studied the floor. His companion squinted at Bodhi. Then he snapped his fingers.

"I know you. You're one of the guys from that greasy burger shack in Clarkburg."

"Clarksville," Bodhi said. "And yes. I was at Billy's Burgers when you drove up last night. I saw you again this morning. You drove past me in your Jaguar."

"Through-hikers, huh?" Diana's tone was frosty.

The man spread his hands wide and smiled broadly. "Okay, guilty as charged. Sorry for the subterfuge. But we really do want to help. We're big fans of Ms. Westin's work. And everybody wants the same thing, right? To find her and bring her back safely."

Bodhi wondered if that was true. From the expression on Diana's face, she had doubts of her own. But before anyone could respond, Aaron bounded over with an armload of equipment.

Oblivious to the undercurrent of tension, he began listing the items he'd gathered. "Everyone needs a headlamp, rain shell, water bottle, and some energy bars. I've got maps of the area and emergency whistles, too."

Sadie looked up from the till. "For the record, this is a bad idea. It'll be full dark soon if it's not already. The trail's not safe at night without proper equipment."

"Then we'd better hurry," Diana said.

Aaron returned with more gear to distribute. His movements were quick and efficient, but his gaze kept returning to Rory's messenger bag and, each time, a muscle tensed in his jaw.

"Headlight?" Aaron asked Bodhi, extending one toward him.

"I have my own," Bodhi replied, patting his backpack. "But thank you."

Undaunted, Aaron held out a first aid kit. "Here. This has everything—bandages, disinfectant, trauma shears, even a tourniquet."

"That's very helpful. Thank you." Bodhi took the

case he offered even though he had a well-stocked first aid kit of his own. The young man was clearly eager to feel useful.

Aaron turned toward Diana, wide-eyed. "We have to find her. She's so special ... I couldn't bear it if ..." His cheeks reddened as he tripped over his words. Then he trailed off for good as Sadie strode over, keys in hand.

She stared at Aaron for a long moment. He didn't meet her eyes.

She exhaled loudly. "Let's go," she said briskly. "I've locked up the register and put the 'Closed' sign up."

As Aaron jogged off alongside Sadie, Diana whispered to Bodhi, "Sadie and Aaron are a couple. They were taking a break when Rory moved to town. She and Aaron had a few dates and, apparently, he has a lingering crush. You may have noticed."

"It seems Sadie is aware of it, too."

Diana nodded. "She is."

"Unresolved emotions can cloud judgment, especially in a crisis situation," he observed.

The former police chief nodded again. "True. Something to bear in mind."

Then she turned to the two men. "We're not in a position to turn down help. So if you want to join us, you may. Do you have names?"

"I'm Tripp Davidson," the older man said immediately.

"Lucas Hamilton," his companion said.

As the others introduced themselves, Diana leaned close to Bodhi and murmured, "I don't like it, but I also want to keep them in sight. Whatever they're up to, I'd rather know than be surprised."

20

Sadie touched Diana lightly on her upper arm.

"Could I have a word with you?"

Diana nodded and jerked her head toward the corner of the shop by the dressing rooms while the others packed up the gear Aaron passed out.

"What is it, Sadie?"

"I know I said this was a bad idea. I misspoke. This is a *terrible* idea."

Diana smiled. She appreciated bluntness. She didn't have time for women—and in her experience, it was almost always women—who sugar-coated what they had to say, worried about hurt feelings or how they'd be perceived. Apparently neither did Sadie.

"It's a terrible idea because we've got a group of untrained searchers who are going to wander out into the woods in the dark?" Diana guessed.

"Well, yes. But also, you don't know any of these men." She waved a hand toward Tripp, Lucas, and Bodhi.

She was right about the fake hikers. But Diana

tried to ease her worry about Bodhi. "You weren't at Vines & Vibes, so you didn't meet him, but Bodhi is a forensic pathology consultant based out of Pittsburgh."

"So he says."

"I've actually heard of him." Diana hadn't mentioned this fact to Dr. King, but she shared it now with Sadie. "When I was still the chief, I used to go to a conference of small town police chiefs every year. The chief from a parish in Louisiana and the chief of a rural town in Illinois were talking about him at dinner. He's somewhat famous in law enforcement circles for determining the cause of unexplained deaths."

Bodhi's credentials didn't have the effect Diana had hoped.

Sadie's voice went shrill. "He wanders around the country solving puzzling deaths? That's a great cover for a serial killer. Maybe *he's* the cause of all these deaths. Did you ever think of that?"

Diana gestured toward Bodhi, who was helping Julie fit a silver emergency blanket into her pack.

"You think *he's* a serial killer?"

Sadie shrugged. "I'm just saying it's awfully convenient that he shows up in small towns where there are deaths and solves them."

"I say this with love: you have *got* to stop listening to true crime podcasts."

The store manager snorted. "Okay. Forget about him. What about those other two?"

Diana couldn't vouch for Tripp and Lucas, but she said, "You're right. We don't know what their agenda is. Under ideal circumstances, I wouldn't bring them along. But we need the help. And let's not pretend everyone else has the purest of motives for joining the search. Julie can't be thrilled that Rory documented the demolition of the Hudson house. She's probably coming along to do damage control. And it's an open secret that there's bad blood between you and Rory."

"It's not bad blood," Sadie protested. "I have nothing against her."

Diana snorted. "Please."

"I'm serious. My beef isn't with her." Sadie's eyes flicked to Aaron.

As a rule, Diana didn't give unsolicited advice. But she'd been where Sadie was, so she made an exception. "Look, Aaron's charming. Everyone loves him. He's friendly, a great guy. You know who else everyone says is a great guy? Ron. They appointed him as police chief because, and I quote, he's the kind of man you'd want to have a beer with. That may be so, but it didn't make him a great partner. And I mean that both as someone who worked with him for twenty-odd years and as someone who was married to him for even longer."

"Aaron's not Ron." Sadie's nostrils flared. She clearly didn't appreciate the comparison.

"I'm not saying he is. I'm only trying—"

"—Let's focus." She gestured toward the men.

Diana shook her head. She'd tried. Some people had to learn the hard way.

"I was the chief of police for a long time, Sadie. Turning in the badge doesn't mean I turned in my instincts."

Sadie opened her mouth and then closed it.

"Listen, my vision may be poor, but I go to the

firing range every weekend. Center mass on an adult man is a pretty big target. Hard to miss, even for me."

"Do you have your gun with you?" Sadie asked in an undertone.

"Of course."

Sadie blew out a breath. "I'd still feel better if we were doing this in the daylight."

"We can't wait. If Rory's seriously injured, she could be dead by morning."

21

Somewhere in the darkness

Rory's eyelids fluttered open. Her head throbbed with each beat of her heart, and for a moment, she couldn't remember where she was. Complete darkness greeted her, thick and disorienting. She strained to focus but couldn't see anything, not even shadows.

"Hello?" She croaked in a raspy whisper.

No response.

She reached up to touch her aching head and connected with something wet and sticky that was matting her hair. She pulled her hand away and caught a whiff of the metallic scent of blood. A fragment of a memory flashed through her mind: the cave, someone calling her name, a sensation of falling.

But where was she now? Not in the cave. Not in the woods.

The surface beneath her wasn't hard, cold stone. She reached down and ran her hands along it. Worn, rough-hewn floorboards. She inhaled. Instead of earth and decaying plant matter, she smelled stale air. She listened, but didn't hear the faint rustle of leaves or the familiar nocturnal birdsongs. She heard the creaks of a house settling.

"Hello?" she called again, still faint, still hoarse.

There was still no answer.

She lifted her head slowly and tried to push herself upright, bracing her palms against the floor. The world spun wildly, and nausea rolled through her in a violent wave. She turned her head to the side just before she retched, bringing up nothing but bile that burned her throat.

When the heaving subsided, she gasped and coughed.

Spent, she rounded her shoulders and hugged her midsection. The dull cramping in her abdomen was sharpening, turning into a hot, needle-like stabbing. Her arms and feet tingled. The tang of metal filled her mouth.

"No, no, no," she moaned as the reality of her situation sunk in.

It had been nearly a year since her last episode. She'd been careful—regular meals, limiting alcohol, managing stress. But the past few days, she'd been busy. First, focused on her exhibition, then upset by the cancellation, and finally caught up in making her statement. She hadn't eaten a proper meal in days. The adrenaline and stress had been constant. And, as she did the math, her stomach sank with the realization that her cycle had aligned perfectly with the worst possible timing.

Her hands shook as she patted her pockets, hoping against hope that she had her phone. Her right hand hit something solid. As she eased the mobile out of her thigh pocket, she would have wept with relief if she hadn't been so dehydrated.

She was going to be okay. Call 911. Then stay calm. That's all she had to do. She raised the phone to her face to activate the facial recognition feature and turn it on. Nothing happened. Too dark probably. She felt for the power button on the side on the phone, and as her hand slid over the glass, the phone bent under the weight of her fingers. The glass was crushed, smashed and caved in. Her heart lurched. Her stomach heaved. No.

She continued to move her hands over the phone in the darkness. The bottom edge was twisted, a chunk of the frame missing entirely. A piece of plastic dangling loosely from the side. She pounded at the side of the phone with her finger, pressing the dead power button over and over, refusing to believe the truth. The phone was destroyed. Useless.

The tears she thought her body couldn't create filled her eyes, and she released the dead phone from her hand. As it hit the floor, she let out a raw sob.

She had no phone. No glucose tablets or carb-rich snacks. No water.

A burst of images flashed through her mind: photographs hanging from her ceiling, Julie standing in rubble, Lydia watching her home being destroyed, Sadie scowling at her across a coffee shop table, kids playing soccer in the Patch. The pictures came fast, disconnected, and jumbled. Her exhibition. The trail. The messenger bag. The cave.

Someone had followed her to the cave. Who? A face hovered just out of reach in her memory.

Trying to puzzle it out made her head throb even worse. The twisting pain in her stomach intensified, a warning sign of what was to come if she didn't get help soon. She eased herself onto her back again, her movements slow and deliberate, and closed her eyes against the darkness.

Without intervention, she had, at best, a few hours before things got much, much worse. She'd only experienced one truly severe attack before—three years ago in Arizona. The memory of that terrifying episode was seared into her brain: the paralyzing pain, the confusion that made her think she was going mad, the seizure that had finally led to her diagnosis.

She needed to focus. But between the pain in her belly and the throbbing in her head, she couldn't. She touched her bloodied skull. She had a head injury. What if it was a concussion?

Exhaustion pulled at her, tempting her back into unconsciousness. She fought it. You weren't supposed to sleep with a head injury, were you? But the darkness was so complete, so enveloping, it made little difference whether her eyes were open or closed.

She shivered and wrapped her arms around herself.

Her thoughts cleared briefly and she remembered the photographs hanging from her apartment ceiling. Her statement about displacement. Forcing the community to understand and acknowledge what was being lost in the name of progress.

Now she was the one who was lost. Displaced. The irony wasn't lost on her, even in her compromised state. She choked out a bitter laugh before she surrendered to sleep.

22

———

On the Great Allegheny Passage

Sadie and Julie drove the ten miles to the trailhead closest to the cave. Evan sat in the passenger seat of Julie's Mercedes, Bodhi folded himself into the back seat, and the others piled into Sadie's three-row SUV. The trip was short and, at least in Julie's car, silent.

They parked and tumbled out of the vehicles. Sadie and Diana must've spent the drive discussing strategy. The former police chief clapped her hands together to draw everyone's attention.

"We're going to use a classic bike wheel model search," Diana announced. "It's what a formal search and rescue team would do if Chief Mercer had seen fit to call one in. Sadie's volunteered with S & R for years, so she's gonna take the lead on determining our search area and priority."

Diana stepped back, and Sadie cleared her throat.

Before she could begin, Julie piped up. "I don't

know what that means—a bike wheel model. And I doubt I'm the only one."

Sadie gave her a brisk nod. "Right. You don't need to understand the nitty gritty. It's just one method used to organize the initial search. People who are lost in the woods tend to follow predictable behaviors. Most folks are found within three hours if you take a few minutes to think through which direction they're likely to have gone and how far. There are lots of variables—children, people with dementia, intoxicated people all exhibit different patterns. So we imagine a bike wheel. The person's last known location is the axle of our bike wheel. It's in the center of the search area."

"So the cave?" Julie's tone was uncertain.

"Exactly. The rim of the wheel is the outer bounds of our initial search. There are mathematical models that we can use to establish the containment area. But gut instinct works, too. Rory's generally fit and healthy. But she's injured, she doesn't have her bike or pack, and she's wearing one shoe. So we'll assume she didn't get far. Let's call it two miles, tops."

"And we're currently two miles east of the cave," Diana added. "So this spot is within the outer bounds of our search area."

"So, we start here?" Evan asked.

"Sort of," Sadie hedged. "We should concentrate our efforts closer to the cave—the axel— and radiate out from there. The model has a hub, which is the immediate area around the cave."

"I did search about a quarter-mile radius around the cave," Bodhi offered.

Diana nodded. "We'll spread out and do it again, though. She may not be stationary."

Sadie went on, "The spokes are established routes leading from the cave—so the trail in both directions, the road, the river, drainage trenches, that sort of thing. We'll radiate out to those. The final part of the model is the reflectors. These are places within the search area where there's a high probability she would go. Places she intended to photograph, water sources, that sort of thing." She turned to Aaron. "Pull up the photos she posted before she went dark. Where did she already go?"

He fumbled with his phone, scrolling. "Uh, in reverse order, the old barn, the unmaintained spur just about a mile from here, the bus shelter up on the road near the scenic overlook, and that abandoned gas station just outside of town."

"Thanks. She might backtrack, but we're going use those locations to predict other locations, close to the cave, where she might have gone next. We'll check the abandoned barn on our way because it's really close to the cave. Then we'll fan out. Let's get going." She hoisted her pack onto her back and set off on the trail.

Bodhi and Diana waited for the others to follow Sadie, then trailed slightly behind the rest of the search party as they made their way west on the trail. This portion of the path was well-maintained, but it narrowed in sections, forcing them to proceed in a loosely organized single file. Sadie led the way with Aaron close behind her, holding his flashlight at an angle that illuminated her footsteps. Julie followed them, then Tripp and Lucas, with Evan just ahead of Bodhi and Diana.

The group had fallen into a natural rhythm, feet crunching on the packed gravel surface of the trail. Occasional snippets of hushed conversation drifted on the air in the otherwise quiet night.

As the trail curved slightly, Evan slowed his pace and fell back to join them.

"Diana, could I have a word?" he asked.

"Of course. You can talk in front of Bodhi."

Evan's gaze flicked to Bodhi, assessing. He hesitated for a moment before plunging in.

"While Chief Ron is famously cynical," he began, choosing his words carefully, "he might have a point about Rory's disappearance."

Diana stiffened beside Bodhi. "You think she staged it to draw attention to her exhibit?"

"I think she believes deeply in what she's documenting. The displacement, the erasure of communities. She'd do almost anything to make people see it."

"Including leaving her own blood in a cave?" Bodhi asked.

Evan grimaced. "No. The blood's what got me thinking. She already had people buzzing after she posted her artist's statement online. All she needed to do was take some photos on the trail and upload them, like she said she would. A stunt like this is unnecessary for her goals. But she's not the only one who stands to benefit from her DIY installation going viral."

"Who are you talking about?" Bodhi asked.

The history professor sighed. "I didn't want to say anything, but I think I have to. That man, Tripp, isn't just a fan of Rory's work. He owns the Hot Metal Art Gallery."

Bodhi stopped walking. "Are you sure?"

"Positive."

"He's the one who canceled her show?" Diana asked.

"Exactly. And trust me, a publicity stunt is more in line with his ethos than Rory's."

"How well do you know him?"

"I don't know him at all. But I do know what led to the show being canceled. Rory came to see me yesterday. She told me Tripp didn't think the show was generating enough buzz, so her ex-boyfriend suggested Rory shoot a series of nude self-portraits to include in the exhibit. She refused, and Tripp said he'd cancel the show if she didn't do it. She told him to shove it."

Bodhi processed this information.

"Tripp is her ex-boyfriend?"

"No." Evan shook his head. "She said her ex and Tripp were close friends."

Diana resumed walking. Her bobbing headlamp lit up Tripp and Lucas from behind.

"Lucas," she said suddenly. "Not long after she moved here, she mentioned an ex who she dated when she was a model. He was a fashion photographer, and he was shooting the Met Gala. He was in a clip from the red carpet that was on the TV in the dentist's office. She announced to the whole waiting room that he was a weasel."

"When did she post about the exhibit?" Bodhi asked.

"This morning." Evan said. "But if you saw them last night on the trail, they were already on their way here. So that's not why they came."

"Maybe they were coming to try to convince her in person to do the nude self-portraits," Diana said slowly. "Maybe they even talked to her and were headed back to Pittsburgh when the news broke about her online statement. And now, they probably figure a missing photographer is almost as good as a naked one for generating buzz."

Evan was right. With Rory missing, Tripp could capitalize on the notoriety of her DIY showing. She wouldn't be able to stop him.

"It's a theory," Bodhi agreed. "But that's all it is—a theory."

"How do we prove it?" Evan asked.

"Easy. We ask Tripp and Lucas."

"Just ... ask them?"

Bodhi nodded. "You'd be surprised what people will tell you if you ask."

23

When they reached a spot about a mile shy of the cave, Sadie halted and everyone behind her stopped walking, too.

Diana peered around, getting her bearings. Then she called, "The abandoned barn Rory photographed is about a third of a mile off the trail, up on the rise. Evan and Aaron, you two break off and search the area leading to the barn and the barn itself. The rest of you spread out and search along the trail."

Evan nodded, pleased to be tasked with the first high probability area. Aaron bopped along beside him, full of energy.

"Are you from Union Hill, originally?" Evan asked as they picked over the rocks and tree branches to make their way up the hill.

Aaron was careful to shine the light low, which Evan appreciated. He wasn't really an outdoorsman. He was more of a sit in the library with a book and a brandy man.

"Yes sir, born and bred."

"Do you ever think about moving away?" Evan was always curious to hear the answer when he spoke to young people who had stayed in the area.

"No, never. Why would I? The trails are here, clean air, there's good fishing in the summertime. It's beautiful. And with all the investment and buildings that Julie's bringing in, everything I want is here. And what I can't get here, I can just go down to Pittsburgh for."

Evan got it. As Rory had said, there were winners and losers in the revitalization. And apparently this young man felt at least that he was a winner.

"Do you like your work?"

Aaron's expression tightened. "It's a job. Like my dad always said, it's not supposed to be fun. That's why they call it work. I just kind of wish I didn't work for such a big corporation."

Evan cocked his head.

OAC had a reputation for being one of the best employers in the country, right up there with REI and Patagonia in the outdoor adventure space. Sure, they were big companies, but they were certified B corporations. All three offered good benefits, progressive policies, and generous pay.

"Really?" he asked.

"I mean, it's fine." The young man huffed out a breath and shook his head. "It's just, Sadie's my manager."

"Ah, the young woman who organized the search party."

"Right. She's also my girlfriend."

That wasn't really a corporate issue. Or was it? "There's no prohibition about the two of you dating?"

"No, but because Sadie's in management, she had to disclose it to human resources. And you'd think she'd cut me some slack since we're dating. But I guess she feels like *she's* under a microscope, so she's got *me* under a microscope. If I come in a couple minutes late, she writes me up. If my drawer's short, she files a report. She never just lets anything slide."

Evan considered this. "Well, she may be trying to do everything on the straight and narrow because you're dating, or it could just be her personality. Some people are cut out to be cogs in a wheel."

"Cogs in a wheel," he repeated. "Yeah. Sadie's a cog."

"Others, like you perhaps, and certainly like me, are more free-spirited. We see the flaws in the system. We can navigate it, and we can live within it, but it constrains us."

"But you're the history center director. You *are* the system."

He smiled. "Ah. Am I? Perhaps. I choose programming at the center that I think will raise questions about the powers that be. I also teach a history course at the college about American protest movements. Much of it focuses on workers' rights. I think you'd find it interesting."

"Yeah?"

"You could audit it."

Aaron made a face.

Evan went on, "Or not. You could read. There are also podcasts and YouTube channels devoted to the subject. I'd be happy to give you a list." He checked his phone discreetly, noting the time. Still early. He pocketed it and continued scanning the ground.

Casually, he said, "You know, what Rory's doing is a form of protest."

"The exhibit? I guess. I mean, she's showing the darker side of capitalism and revitalization and stuff."

"Yes, that, but also her disappearance."

"What do you mean?"

Evan paused. "She said she was going to shine a light on the displaced. She left her home. She set out on the trail. That was to bring attention to the issue and to her work."

"Right? And?"

"Well, what better way to bring even more attention to it than to go off the grid, to vanish? It would keep people talking."

Even in the shadows of the light, Evan could see that this did not land well with Aaron. The vein in his neck tightened, popped out, and his jaw ticked.

"Are you saying she disappeared on purpose? This is a stunt? Did she plant that blood for us to find?" He was spiraling.

Evan wanted Aaron to question the situation, not melt down. "Son, let's sit for a moment." He guided him to a fallen log. "Take some slow breaths. You seem very distressed."

Aaron gripped his knees and took several gulping breaths before he looked up, tears shining in his eyes. "I really care about Rory. If you know something, please tell me."

Evan studied the young man for a very long time. "Are you and Rory ... involved?"

"Not anymore. We dated for a while when she first moved to Union Hill. Sadie and I were taking a break.

But Rory decided she didn't want anything serious. She wanted to focus on her work."

"Ahh." Evan wondered how that idea had sat with Aaron.

As if he'd read Evan's mind, Aaron said, "I understand. Now, I mean. I was pretty hurt at first. But seeing her photography, I get it. It's powerful. Like that picture of Mr. Kovalic on his porch, the one hanging in your history center. I hope she goes back and documents the demolition of his house the way she did for Mrs. Hudson."

Evan cleared his throat, then gave Aaron a bracing clap on the back. "Well, let's go find her, shall we? So she can."

He stood and hurried up the hill toward the barn, away from the eastern ridgeline, where the Kovalic house, the last remaining structure on Company Way, stood lonely and desolate in the distance. After a moment, Aaron trudged behind him.

24

Sadie was off the path, her map spread out on a flat rock and illuminated by a flashlight. Aaron and Evan had reported that the barn was a bust—no sign of Rory. So she carefully drew an x over that spot and studied the containment area. Where would Rory go?

Diana would have some ideas. She wouldn't be able make out the details on the map, not in this light, not with her eyesight. But she knew these woods as well as anyone and had rescued dozens of lost hikers over the years.

Sadie began to fold up her map, planning to consult Diana when she overheard Aaron talking to the former police chief just feet away, down on the trail.

"You know," Aaron was saying, "despite the circumstances, it's nice to be outside after being cooped up inside all day."

"So you were at the shop all day?"

Diana asked the question casually. Maybe too casually. One of Diana's strengths when she'd been the police chief was making suspects so comfortable that they forgot who they were talking to.

Sadie brushed the thought aside. Diana wasn't interrogating Aaron. She was just making conversation.

"Yep. We've been swamped. I didn't even take a real lunch break. I ran out and grabbed a sandwich to eat in the back while I checked in a big order."

Sadie froze.

He was lying. *Why* was he lying?

She'd skipped lunch to take care of the order, not him. Not only had he taken his break, he'd come back late—and empty-handed, after promising to pick something up for her to eat. He told her he'd lost track of time because he'd detoured from the deli to check out the excitement outside Rory's apartment.

She'd blown up at him because he was already on a performance improvement plan. He'd come in late twice last week despite her waking him up and handing him a mug of coffee before she left their place to open the store. Taking a ninety-minute lunch when he already had two strikes was beyond irresponsible. It was almost like he was daring her to fire him. When she pointed this out, he'd begged her to doctor his time record, but she hadn't. So not only was his lie stupid, it was provably false.

Diana and Aaron's voices faded as they walked away. But Sadie leaned back against the rock and worked through her racing thoughts.

What had Aaron being doing for an hour and a

half? Had he gone to Rory's place hoping to run into her?

She knew in her heart that he wasn't over Rory. Their relationship, if you could even call it that, had been brief. More like a fling. But when Rory walked into a room, Aaron lit up. Sometimes she caught him watching Rory with longing in his eyes.

Big deal, he had a crush. That didn't mean he had anything to do with her disappearance.

Her attempt to convince herself fell flat. If that was true, why had he just lied to Diana?

Maybe he was embarrassed about slacking off. Especially after she'd read him the riot act.

But what if there was more to it than that? Ninety minutes was just about enough time to bike the twelve miles to the cave and back. It would be tight, but for a cyclist as fit and experienced as Aaron, it was doable. He probably hadn't. Almost certainly hadn't. But he *could* have.

She should tell Diana. As soon as she had the thought, she dismissed it.

No, she shouldn't. Raising the issue would distract from the search effort. And she didn't *really* believe Aaron had done anything wrong.

Diana's warning about her relationship had her rattled. That was all.

But the twist in her stomach told her she had to say something. She muscled down the whisper of guilt that said she was a disloyal girlfriend. Then she pushed off from the boulder and went down to the trail to find Diana and set the record straight.

But Diana had her head bent down listening to

something Evan was saying, so Sadie called the search party together and told them they had one more mile to go. She could talk to Diana when they reached the cave.

25

B odhi got his chance to talk to Lucas when they finally reached the spot on the trail where he'd spotted Rory's bike. Sadie called for the search party to take a five-minute break before they headed to the cave. They dropped their packs and scattered across the clearing to stretch, make phone calls, and drink some water.

Bodhi made a series of neck circles and stretched his arms overhead before pulling out his canteen. He drifted toward Tripp and Lucas, who were standing a bit apart from the others.

"—didn't expect her to be so dramatic," Tripp was saying. "Business is business."

"She overreacted," Lucas agreed. "She always did have a flair for theatrics. It's not like she's never shown a little skin—"

A clatter drowned out the rest of the sentence. Evan had dropped his metal water bottle, and it bounced off a rock. The two men turned toward the sound and Bodhi used it as an excuse to nod a hello.

Lucas nodded back.

"I gotta drain the snake," Tripp announced loudly before he walked a few feet away and plunged into the trees not far from where the red trail bicycle still sat.

Once Tripp was out of sight, Bodhi edged closer to Lucas, who was rifling through his backpack. He held up an assortment of bars for Bodhi's inspection.

"Which one of these is the least disgusting? You look like you know your way around trail bars."

He leaned in. "The date bar is pretty good. It'll make you thirsty, though."

"Thanks." Lucas ripped the package open and bit off the corner of the dense bar.

"Now, I have a question for you."

Lucas chewed and swallowed before responding. "Yes?"

"You said you and your friend are fans of Aurora Westin's work, right?"

"Uh-huh."

"Aren't you a photographer, as well? A fashion photographer?"

"Yes. You've heard of me?"

Bodhi let him have his moment of pride then he said, "You worked with her when she was a model, right? Didn't the two of you date?"

Lucas stopped chewing but worked his jaw. Finally, he blew out a breath. "Fine, yes, I know her—knew her. I haven't spoken to her in years."

"But your friend owns the gallery that canceled her show."

He grunted a response that Bodhi took as confirmation.

"Why are you and Mr. Davidson really here?"

Before he could respond, Tripp returned, zipping his fly. Sensing the tension, he said, "What's going on?"

"They know," Lucas told him sourly.

Tripp glanced between his friend and Bodhi. "Know what?"

"Did you honestly think nobody would figure out your connection to Rory?"

Tripp snorted, unimpressed. "Fine. Yes, I own the gallery that was going to show Rory's work. And yes, Lucas used to date her. Ancient history. You've got us. We're not random fans. Well done, Dr. King. Or should I call you Dr. Watson?"

He refused to take the bait. "Bodhi's fine. You were in Clarksville last night. Before she unveiled her guerrilla exhibition. Why were you coming to see her?"

"We came to talk some sense into her," Lucas explained.

Tripp scoffed. "Burning a bridge with an established gallery like mine is a mistake that won't go over well in the arts community. As for her little DIY installation, that's nothing more than a childish stunt to get attention."

"Unlike gratuitous nude self-portraits?" He couldn't resist asking the question.

Tripp had the self-awareness to look marginally embarrassed, but he shrugged. "It was a business suggestion. Sex sells. Always has, always will."

"And when she refused?"

"I canceled the show. My gallery, my rules."

"Her reaction was completely outsized," Lucas interjected. "She could have simply said no and negotiated. Instead, she hung her photos from her ceiling and posted them online with some manifesto about displacement."

Bodhi eyed them dispassionately. "That still doesn't explain why you joined the search for her. She already announced that the show was canceled and unveiled her photographs. It's too late to stop her now."

The two men exchanged glances.

"We're here," Tripp said slowly, "because her little stunt is working. Social media's blowing up with her guerrilla exhibit. Art blogs are covering it. My phone's been ringing off the hook with collectors asking about her work."

"We need her," Lucas said. "She's a hot commodity now—nude or clothed."

Bodhi didn't try to hide his surprise at the frank admission. "That's blunt."

Tripp spread his hands. "It's just business. Of course, we're trying to capitalize on her talent."

"Even while she's alone in the woods, possibly seriously injured?"

"That's why we joined the search," Lucas said, as if it were obvious. "We need to find her before something happens to her."

"Or to make sure she's not ever found. I imagine that would increase her market value even more, wouldn't it?"

Tripp's smile thinned into a line. "The idea never crossed my mind."

"And for the record, your accusation is offensive," Lucas added, a warning in his tone.

Bodhi held his gaze steadily. Lucas stepped closer.

From the other side of the clearing, Sadie cupped her hands around her mouth and called, "Break's over. Gather 'round."

Lucas broke eye contact first and followed Tripp past Bodhi, making sure to knock into him with a shoulder as he passed.

26

———————

GAP Mile 92.3, Between Clarksville and Union Hill

"Nobody enter the cave," Diana commanded, taking charge of the scene like it was second nature, which it was. Despite her low vision, which was even more problematic at night, she was the experienced law enforcement officer. She had to lead.

The others assembled in a cluster at the cave's entrance, headlamps creating a chaotic dance of light and shadow on the stone walls. Diana felt the familiar adrenaline surge that came with taking command of a crime scene—because that's what this was until proven otherwise.

Bodhi stepped up beside her and aimed his headlamp at the ground. "This is where I found the blood," he said, indicating the dark stain about ten feet inside the cave entrance.

As he adjusted his light, she heard his sharp intake of breath.

"What?" she asked, trying to make out what had caught his attention.

"Look," he murmured, his voice barely audible.

She followed his finger to the ground but saw only wavy, indistinct shapes—blurred patches of light and darkness that refused to resolve into anything meaningful. She turned her head slightly, using her peripheral vision, but it didn't help. The macular degeneration robbed her of the fine detail she needed, especially in low light.

"What?" she repeated forcefully, frustration edging her tone.

Bodhi leaned closer. "My headlamp has four light settings," he explained as he clicked through them, "white light, red light, blue light, and ultraviolet light."

"Okay, most headlamps have multiple light modes."

"I accidentally clicked one too many times before. I selected the UV mode and the blood is fluorescing under the UV light."

"But, how? You didn't spray luminol or anything." She knew that crime scene investigators used luminol because it interacted with blood to create a blue glow.

"Right, I didn't. And this blood isn't blue. It's glowing a bright orangish-red." He pitched his voice low.

"What does that mean?" Diana dropped her voice to match his near-whisper.

"It could indicate a medical condition called acute intermittent porphyria—AIP. It's quite rare, but one characteristic is that the blood contains porphyrins that fluoresce under UV light."

He waited while she processed this information.

After a moment, she asked, "You think Rory has this condition?"

"It's a possibility. AIP can cause severe abdominal pain, confusion, and even seizures and convulsions in acute attacks. If she's having an episode, combined with what may well be a head injury she could be confused, disoriented, or even delusional."

"A head injury? What are you basing that on?"

"A possible head injury," he clarified. "Based on the amount of blood. Scalp wounds, even minor ones, are notorious for bleeding copiously."

"Before we run off half-cocked let's find out if anyone knows about any health conditions. You asked about her mental health back at the tapas bar, not her physical health. We'll split up and ask the others casually. No need to alarm everyone yet. I'll talk to Julie first."

"I might as well ask Lucas. I've already stirred the hornet's nest," he responded.

Bodhi escorted Diana back to the trail, keeping a light hand on her elbow, then he guided her toward Julie, who stood apart from the group, staring into the darkness beyond the cave.

"I've got it from here, thanks."

He strode off in the other direction.

She carefully walked over to the real estate developer she'd known since childhood. "Julie, do you know if Rory has any medical conditions?"

Julie turned, surprise registering on her face. "Why?"

"It might be relevant to finding her."

Julie hesitated. "I don't know, actually. I've signed for some packages delivered to the apartment when she's been away on shoots. They could have been prescriptions or medical supplies. Or they could've been photography equipment. Or sex toys, for all I know."

Diana wasn't touching the sex toys comment with a six-foot, er, pole. "She never mentioned any health problems, though?"

"No," Julie crossed her arms. "And I would never dream of asking. Rory's very private about certain things."

Diana waited, sensing Julie had more to say.

"We argued last night," Julie volunteered suddenly. "About the Hudson property—the demolition she photographed."

Diana tilted her head. "Why are you telling me this now?"

Julie looked away. "I don't know. Maybe I feel guilty? She was pretty upset. And, honestly, so was I."

"Were you upset enough to follow her to the cave and confront her?" Diana asked bluntly.

Julie's head snapped back. "Confront her? As in assault her and drag her away? No! Come on, Diana, what kind of person do you think I am?"

"The kind who sometimes puts profit over people," Diana replied evenly. "I've watched Union Hill change under your guidance. Not all of it for the better."

"Now you sound like her."

Diana let the retort hang on the air.

After a moment, Julie protested further, "I create opportunities. I can't help who gets left behind."

"Can't you?"

Julie's voice hardened. "I didn't hurt Rory. I wouldn't. For all our disagreements, I actually like her."

Diana nodded, letting the subject drop. "If you think of anything about her health, let me know."

She moved away, cautiously, keeping her gaze on the pool of light created by her headlamp. As she did so, she wondered what had prompted Julie's voluntary admission about the argument. Guilty conscience? Or was she trying to get ahead of something?

Before Diana had gone ten feet, Julie was making a phone call. The harsh glow of her phone lit up the dark.

As Diana turned toward Sadie and Aaron, who were across the clearing, Julie said in a throaty voice, "Ron? Do you have a minute?"

Diana froze, then melted into the copse of trees to listen to Julie's end of the conversation.

"Nothing so far. Except being grilled by your ex." She laughed lightly at something Ron said. Then, "Don't worry. She doesn't suspect anything."

There was a pause while Julie inspected her manicure. "Of course I'm sure. She wouldn't recognize the truth if it rang her doorbell."

Diana clenched her hands into fists and pressed her lips together. She couldn't explode on Julie even though her entire body was tense, waiting for her to unload. She had to keep her temper in check and gather more information.

"I will. Yes, as soon as I'm out of these blasted woods." Julie paused, listening. "Well, I had to volunteer to come along. It would have looked suspicious if I hadn't." She ended the call.

Julie stepped out from between the trees. "You and Ron are in on this together? The two of you are responsible for Rory's disappearance?"

At the sound of her voice, Julie started. She turned and gaped at Diana, lit up by the beam of the headlamp Diana wore.

"It's not what it sounds like."

Diana laughed without humor. "Really? Because it sounds like you and the chief of police conspired to get rid of the activist artist who was bringing negative attention to your economic development projects."

"No, you misinterpreted—"

"My opinion of my ex-husband is exceedingly low. But apparently, I've been giving him too much credit. I knew he was lazy and complacent. But corrupt? That's a new—"

"Diana, stop." Julie's voice was raw. "Just stop. We're not co-conspirators. We're lovers."

A wave of shock rolled over Diana like ice water. "What?" She forced the syllable out from her tightening throat.

"Ron and I are together. We're a couple. I'm sorry you had to find out this way. Ron didn't want you to find out at all. We didn't want to hurt you by adding insult to injury."

"How long?" Diana croaked.

Julie drew a deep breath. "Not while you were still married. It was after. He was struggling after your diagnosis. He needed a friend, some support."

"He needed support after my diagnosis?" She knew she was screeching, but she didn't care. "No, Julie. I needed support. I could have used a friend."

Julie's face sagged. "Diana—"

"No. Forget it." Diana tamped down her anger and hurt and studied the woman she'd known for four decades. Then she shook her head. "You could do better than Ron. You deserve better than him."

Julie gave her a small, sad smile. "I don't see him the same way you do."

After a moment, Diana turned without another word and crossed the clearing to where Sadie stood studying the map. Aaron hovered nearby, waiting for his girlfriend/boss to give him a task. She would deal with the betrayal and sheer rage roiling through her later. She had a job to do now.

"Either of you know if Rory has any health problems?" she asked casually as she joined them.

Sadie shook her head without looking up from the map. "No idea. We're not exactly friends."

An understatement if there ever was one, Diana thought.

Aaron remained conspicuously silent.

"Aaron?" Diana prompted.

He glanced at her, then quickly away. "Not really."

Diana waited. Years of interrogation had taught her the power of silence.

Sure enough, after a moment, Aaron jerked his head toward the trees and walked off in that direction. Diana gave him a thirty-second head start.

Before she could follow him, Sadie stowed her map and said, "I need to tell you something."

Her somber tone made Diana forget about Aaron for the moment. "What is it?

"Aaron lied to you about where he was this afternoon."

27

"Now what?" Lucas demanded as Bodhi walked up to him.

Bodhi raised his hands in a conciliatory gesture. "I need to ask you something about Rory."

"I already told you. I didn't attack her in that cave." He spat the words.

Bodhi took a centering breath and said, "The blood in the cave has unusual properties. It suggests a rare, and serious, medical condition. If Rory has this condition, we need to know. It could be critical to finding her alive."

Lucas gave him a skeptical look. "What kind of medical condition?"

"One that makes her blood glow," Bodhi explained.

He scoffed. "Glow in the dark blood? Sounds like science fiction."

"It's not. It's a documented symptom of a rare, potentially fatal, disorder."

"Well, I haven't been with Rory in years and when

we were together her blood didn't glow." He turned on his heel and walked away.

Bodhi was about to follow him, when Aaron grabbed his arm. His eyes were wild.

"I heard what you said. Diana asked me the same question. I thought she was going to come down here so we could talk, but Sadie's yammering at her. And I don't want to say this in front of Sadie."

"You don't want to say what?" Bodhi pitched his voice low in an effort to calm the frantic man.

Aaron blew out a shaky breath. "I saw a bottle of pills in Rory's bathroom. The one time I, you know, spent the night. I asked her about it, and she got weird and defensive. Shut me down completely."

"Do you remember the name of the medication?" It was a long shot, but Bodhi had to ask.

Aaron rubbed the back of his neck. "As a matter of fact, I do. Because the whole thing was weird. They were only glucose tablets. Which is no big deal, right? But like I said, she was *really* upset that I'd seen them. I think it's part of why she ended things with me."

Bodhi met his eyes. "Thanks, Aaron."

"Does that mean she has it? The glowing blood thing?"

"It might."

Aaron blanched. "We have to find her."

Just then, Diana called down to them, "Bodhi, could you come up here? I'd come to you, but that's a steep downhill and the ground's uneven."

He excused himself and went to join Diana.

"What did you learn?" she asked.

"First, I didn't get to tell this bit before. The glowing blood distracted me. Lucas and Tripp admit they came here to convince Rory to work with them again. They want to profit from the attention her guerrilla exhibition is attracting."

"They're vultures," Diana muttered.

"Agreed. But I don't really believe they harmed her. They need her alive and working. And Lucas says he doesn't know about any medical conditions."

"Hmm. Neither do Sadie and Julie. Although I did find out that Julie's involved with my ex-husband. And Sadie told me Aaron lied about where he was this afternoon."

He blinked at her, and she went on. "I know, that doesn't have anything to do with Rory's health. But it is further evidence that everyone in the search party has a secret."

"Let's leave that aside for now. Aaron saw glucose tablets in Rory's bathroom. He says he asked her about them, and she got agitated."

She shook her head. "Glucose tablets? Does that mean anything."

"Glucose could be used to prevent or treat an AIP episode at home. The gold standard is hemin, but that's injected intravenously, and it's eye-poppingly expensive. Most people manage their porphyria through diet and lifestyle. I suspect that's what Rory does—if she has AIP, that is."

"Are there any glucose pills in her messenger bag?" Diana asked.

"No."

She was silent for a moment. Then she asked. "Hypothetically, if she's having an acute episode and she injured her head, how serious is it?"

He didn't sugarcoat it. "Hypothetically, it could be fatal."

Diana straightened her shoulders. "Then we need to find her. Tonight."

"We need to think like Rory. She came here for a reason. The message of her exhibition was about displacement, about people being pushed aside."

She twitched her lips to the side. "So, presumably she'd go somewhere significant to her theme, right?"

"It's a reasonable assumption. One caveat though: if she's having an AIP attack, she may not be thinking rationally."

"We have to start somewhere," Diana said firmly. "We're running out of time. We'll skip all the spokes in the bike wheel model and focus on the reflectors. It's what my gut's telling me to do."

"Then that's what we'll do."

28

Diana gathered the search party in a tight circle. Seven faces illuminated by headlamps looked back at her awaiting her direction. She straightened her shoulders, calling on decades of law enforcement experience.

"We need to split up to cover more ground," she announced. "Time isn't on our side."

Bodhi stepped forward. "I agree. Based on what we've learned, Rory may be experiencing a medical emergency in addition to any injuries she sustained."

"What kind of medical emergency?" Evan asked, his voice tight with concern.

Diana and Bodhi exchanged a glance before Bodhi answered. "We believe she may have a rare condition called acute intermittent porphyria. During an attack, she would experience severe abdominal pain, nausea, and potentially confusion or even hallucinations."

"Lord," Tripp muttered. "I had no idea."

"None of us did," Julie said. "She's very private."

"How do we help her if we find her?" Sadie asked, practical as always.

"Glucose can help," Bodhi explained. "Sugar. Anything with carbohydrates. And getting her to medical attention as quickly as possible."

Diana nodded. "Everyone check the food you have. Share anything with sugar—chocolate energy bars, candy, fruit. Distribute it evenly between the groups."

As they rifled through their bags, Diana set out the search plan.

"We'll form three teams. Julie, Sadie, and I will head north to check the rest of the abandoned barns and tunnels. Tripp, Lucas, and Aaron will investigate the remaining caves to the south of the trail. Bodhi and Evan stay here and examine Rory's camera. Go back through her camera roll looking for earlier shots. Look for places that seem meaningful to her. When you find one, call both teams, and whoever is closer will check it out."

Bodhi cocked his head. "Why don't I go with Julie and Sadie? You stay with Evan."

She lifted her chin. "I can manage. And we need you centrally located for when we find her. You're the only one with medical training."

He didn't fight her. She was right.

She turned to Sadie. "What do you think for a time limit—three hours?"

Sadie nodded. "That's the max. We'll reconvene here in three hours regardless of whether we find her."

"What if we don't?" Lucas asked.

Sadie flicked her eyes toward Diana before answering. Diana nodded.

"We call in the dogs and helicopters."

There was a heavy silence.

Then Diana said, "Stay in radio range. Two miles—three miles max."

"What if one of us finds her?" Aaron asked.

"Three short whistle blasts," Diana instructed. "Then radio your location."

They distributed the supplies—first aid kits, radios, extra batteries for headlamps, and food—then gathered at the edge of the clearing.

"Let's move out," Diana commanded.

The two groups headed out, their six headlamps creating a bright burst of light that gradually separated in two constellations as they peeled off in opposite directions in the dark night.

29

North of the Cave, GAP Mile 93

Diana, Julie, and Sadie picked their way carefully through the underbrush. Julie kept close to Diana's side, occasionally touching her elbow when the terrain grew especially treacherous. Sadie took care to illuminate the ground ahead of Diana with a wide-beamed flashlight. Diana accepted the assistance without argument. Her priority was finding Rory. She'd have plenty of time to indulge her anger at Julie's betrayal later.

"There should be an old rail tunnel about half a mile ahead," Sadie said, consulting her map by headlamp. "And then the two abandoned barns beyond that."

"Perfect hiding places," Julie remarked.

Diana snorted. "Or perfect places to stash a body."

The blunt assessment hung in the air for several

paces before Julie broke the silence. "I can't believe I'm saying this, but I hope it's just a publicity stunt."

"It's not," Diana said firmly. "The blood in that cave was real."

They walked in silence until they reached the tunnel entrance—a dark half-circle of stone emerging from the hillside, covered in moss and vines.

"I'll go first," Sadie volunteered, adjusting her headlamp to its brightest setting.

The three women entered the tunnel, their footsteps echoing against the damp stone walls. Their beams of light swept across the curved ceiling and graffiti-covered walls.

"Rory!" Diana called, her voice bouncing back at them. "Rory Westin!"

Only the slow drip of water hitting the ground answered.

Halfway through the tunnel, Diana stopped suddenly. "Wait. I heard something."

The three women froze, listening intently. A faint rustling came from ahead.

"Rory?" Julie called, her voice hopeful.

A pair of yellow eyes reflected in their headlamps and a raccoon scurried away into a crevice.

They let out three deflated breaths in unison, then continued through the tunnel, emerging on the other side into a small clearing where the moonlight illuminated the silhouettes of two weathered wooden structures.

"The barns," Sadie confirmed.

As they approached the first structure, Julie murmured, "This would make a great event center.

Imagine the weddings, the receptions. The possibilities are endless."

Sadie stiffened. "Do you think you'll ever be satisfied?"

Julie's headlamp beam swung to Sadie's face. "I beg your pardon?"

"It's not a Monopoly board, Julie. You don't have to gobble up all the properties."

"I'm trying to save this town," Julie shot back. "Do you know what Union Hill looked like before I started investing? Boarded-up storefronts. No jobs. Young people fleeing as fast as they could graduate."

"And now the people who stayed can't afford to live there," Sadie retorted.

"That's pretty funny coming from you. Do you think your company would have moved into town without all my improvements? You'd be living someplace else entirely right now."

Diana held up her hand. "Enough sniping at each other," she said in a sharp tone. "Save the debate for after we find Rory."

The other two fell silent as they reached the first barn. Diana pushed open the creaking door, and they aimed their lights around the structure. The interior was empty save for some rotting hay bales and rusted farm equipment.

"Nothing here," Diana concluded. "Let's check the other one."

As they crossed to the second barn, Sadie turned to Julie and said in a softer tone. "You're right. Not about everything, but about OAC. They were planning to open their next store in Colorado until they saw your proposal."

Even in the poor light, Diana saw Julie's face brighten with pride.

Sadie's voice faltered as she went on. "Although maybe that would have been better for me, personally."

Julie flashed Diana a look, and silent understanding passed between them.

"If there's one thing I've learned the hard way," Julie said bluntly. "It's not to make career decisions based on my romantic relationships. And believe me, I did learn it the hard way."

"Me, too," Diana added.

Sadie shook her head. "I know Aaron and I would be better off as friends. Our relationship is on borrowed time. I just wish he'd pull his act together at work so I could recommend him for a promotion. I don't want to leave OAC in a lurch, but I'd like to move on to what I really want to do."

"Which is?"

"Open my own business specializing in curated off-the-trail bike tours." She laughed dryly. "Focusing on the types of places Rory photographs—places like this." She waved a hand at the barn they were approaching.

"That's a great idea," Julie told her. "It's an unusual offering that will draw people to town. I can help you craft a proposal."

The younger woman blew out a breath and shook her head. "I owe it to OAC to leave the store in good hands. I've had an internal posting for a manager up company-wide for three months. But, even with all the development, it's a hard sell to get someone to relocate to Union Hill. My regional manager wants me to promote from within. Since Aaron's my only employee, that means him."

"Ahhh." Now Diana understood.

"Have you told him?" Julie asked. "Maybe he'd get it together if he knew you were considering him as your replacement. He's great with people."

"He is. But he's been on a performance improvement plan, and now with him lying about where he was this afternoon ... I should probably fire him, not promote him." She kicked at the path with the toe of her boot, and a cloud of dust rose.

They reached the second barn, which, against all odds, was in worse condition than the first. Half the roof had collapsed, leaving the interior exposed to the elements.

"Rory!" Julie called as they entered cautiously.

"Be careful where you step," Sadie warned, testing a floorboard with her foot.

They searched the barn thoroughly, finding nothing but an abandoned animal den and some dusty beer cans left behind years ago by partying teenagers who were probably parents themselves by now.

"Now what?" Julie asked, shining her light around.

"There's a springhouse on the property. We might as well check that, too," Diana answered wearily. "And then hope the other team is having better luck than we are."

30

Cave Clearing, GAP Mile 92.3

Bodhi removed Rory's digital camera from her messenger bag. Evan peered over his shoulder as he pressed the button to power it on. The camera came to life, illuminating their faces in the darkness.

Bodhi navigated to the image review function and began scrolling through the photos. The most recent shots showed the photos she'd uploaded earlier from the trail. Then shots of the impromptu exhibition in her living room—judging by the perspective, she'd taken them from the deck of the tapas bar. He continued to scroll back. Julie surveying the rubble of a demolished house, a series of photos documenting the destruction, and a series of its owner standing in her kitchen one last time.

"These are from two days ago," Evan volunteered unnecessarily.

Bodhi continued backward through the images until he found a sequence of shots taken earlier. Landscapes of the trail, close-ups of wildflowers, a dilapidated vegetable stand on the side of the road, and then—

"What's this?" He stopped on an image of a massive brick structure partly reclaimed by nature. Vines crawled up its walls, windows were broken or boarded, but the imposing edifice remained intact.

Evan leaned closer. "That's the old Allen & Sons factory."

Bodhi swiped to see more images of the building from different angles.

"It was a garment manufacturer back in the early 1900s," Evan explained, his voice taking on the cadence of a lecturer. "Young women, mostly immigrants, made dresses for wealthy Pittsburghers. After the Triangle Shirtwaist Factory fire in New York in 1911, the workers here organized a walkout to protest their own unsafe conditions."

Bodhi studied a close-up image of faded lettering above the factory entrance. "She took a lot of photos of this place."

"It's the perfect embodiment of her displacement theme," Evan said, growing animated. "A site of worker exploitation, resistance, and then abandonment. It sits less than half a mile from the trail but has never been renovated or recognized historically because it doesn't have the scenic value developers like Julie are looking for."

Bodhi swiped through more images, finding interior shots of the factory—cavernous rooms with broken sewing machines, dust-covered worktables, and shafts of light streaming through holes in the ceiling.

"These were taken earlier in the week," Bodhi noted, checking the date on the timestamps.

Evan nodded eagerly. "We should check the factory."

Bodhi frowned. "We need to stay here. We'll radio the others."

Before he could, static crackled, then Aaron's voice came across the airwaves. "She's not here. We're thinking we'll go down to the drainage ditch and check that. Follow it out toward Company Row and then turn around if we don't find her."

Evan grabbed for the radio. "No, don't. Do you know the old Allen & Sons factory?"

"Yeah. Why?"

"She was just there two days ago. She took a lot of pictures. She may have gone back," Evan explained.

There was a long pause. Then Aaron said. "It's outside the containment area. Out of radio range."

Evan frowned. "Barely. Maybe three miles, at most."

Bodhi held his hand out, and Evan reluctantly placed the radio in it.

"Stand by for a minute, okay?" Bodhi told Aaron.

"Will do."

He eyed Evan. "How sure are you that she'd go to the factory?"

Evan hedged. "It's the logical place to look."

"They're closer to the ditch. If she did follow it, they'll waste a lot of time going in the opposite direction. Time we don't have," Bodhi countered.

Evan opened his mouth to argue just as the radio

crackled to life again. "It's Sadie. We struck out, too. We're closer to the factory. We'll head that way. Aaron, you follow the ditch to Company Row."

"You'll be out of range," Aaron protested.

"We won't be able to reach Bodhi, but make sure your work cell phone is turned on. I'll be able to contact you. Satellite phones," she explained for Bodhi's benefit.

"Over."

Evan lunged for the radio and snatched it with trembling hands. "No, Aaron. Wait. Go to the history center instead. I should have thought of it sooner. She has a key. I gave it to her when we were setting up the *Vanishing Coal Country* exhibit. There's water, electricity. That's where she would have gone."

Aaron's voice came back, excited. "That makes sense. We're on it. Sadie, do you copy?"

"Yes. Do it."

Evan thumbed off the radio and blew out a breath.

Bodhi pulled out his map and unfolded it. He lowered his head to study it, curious how far Aaron was from the history center. But the light from his headlamp was insufficient. He pressed the button to change the mode. He pressed it again, cycling through the UV setting and a flash of red luminescence in the periphery of his vision caught his eye. He swung his head to focus on it. Evan's left shoe glowed with a large red smear.

Evan looked down at it, then up at Bodhi.

"It's ... it's not what you think."

"You have Rory's blood on your shoe. You were with her in the cave."

Evan's shoulders slumped. "It's not what you think," he repeated.

"Then explain," Bodhi said in a measured tone. "Rory is gravely ill. Without intervention, she could die. What happened when you met her in the cave?"

Evan paced, running his hands through his hair. "I didn't hurt her. You have to believe that."

"I do," Bodhi said. "But I need to know what happened."

Evan stopped pacing and faced Bodhi. "She contacted me yesterday morning after her gallery show was canceled. She wanted my help creating an impactful exhibition. Something that couldn't be shut down or compromised."

"Go on," Bodhi prompted when Evan hesitated.

"We came up with the idea of hanging her exhibit and then hitting the trail." Evan swallowed hard. "We talked about her going to the factory. She thought she might spend the night there and get shots in the early morning light. At dawn, when the seamstresses would have been reporting to work way back when."

"How'd she end up in the cave?"

"I guess she stopped to upload some of her photos. I was walking on the trail, trying to get my steps in before I headed into town for dinner. I saw her bike through the trees, the same as you. I found her in the cave. She looked unwell, unsteady on her feet. She fell and hit her head." His voice cracked. "I panicked. I didn't know what to do."

"So you left her there?" Bodhi couldn't keep the incredulity from his voice.

"She was breathing! I checked. That's probably how I got her blood on my shoe. I thought she'd be fine. I went to town and waited for her to post on social media. She did, and I thought that meant all was well, but I guess she uploaded the photos before I saw her." Tears welled in his eyes. "Then you showed up with her bag and said she was missing. I swear I don't know where she is now."

Bodhi studied him. His face was slick with sweat despite the night chill, and his skin was flushed. His chest rose and fell rapidly. He tugged at his collar.

"Are you okay?"

Evan panted. "Dizzy. Chest ... tight."

Bodhi took the radio from the man's clammy hands and eased him down to the ground, resting his back against a boulder. He crouched and unzipped Evan's jacket, then unbuttoned the top two buttons of his shirt. Evan looked at him with panic in his eyes.

"You're having a heart attack," Bodhi told him in a measured voice. "I've got you."

He picked up the radio. "Aaron? Sadie? I need one of you to call 911. Evan's having a heart attack."

Sadie responded first. "I'll make the call. Aaron, you three are closer to the trailhead. Head over there to meet the paramedics and lead them to the cave."

"We'll keep looking for Rory," a man said. Bodhi couldn't tell whether it was Tripp or Lucas.

"No," Sadie's voice was firm. "You don't know where you're going. Stay with Aaron. We don't need another lost hiker."

Bodhi set the radio aside and returned his attention to Evan. "Try to stay calm. Help is on the way."

He unzipped his pack and took out the first aid kit. "I'm going to give you an aspirin. I need you to chew and swallow it. It'll prevent any blood clots from getting bigger. You're not allergic are you?"

Evan didn't answer. Bodhi looked up and dropped the aspirin. Evan's eyes were rolled back, and his slack body was slumped to the side.

He shook Evan's shoulder. "Evan? Can you hear me?"

No response.

He pressed two fingers to the man's neck, searching for a carotid pulse. Nothing. His chest rose and fell with irregular, gasping breaths that quickly faded to stillness. It sounded as if he was choking and snorting.

"Agonal breathing. Cardiac arrest," Bodhi muttered, positioning Evan flat on his back. He placed the heel of one hand on the center of Evan's chest, covered it with his other hand, and began compressions. He counted under his breath, pushing down two inches with each compression.

As a forensic pathologist, he'd dealt with death daily. But this was different. His patients came to him dead. He didn't lose them. And he wouldn't lose Evan.

One minute passed. Two. Five. His shoulders burned, sweat dripping onto Evan's still face. Bodhi paused only to check for a pulse at the carotid artery. Nothing. He resumed compressions immediately.

"Come on, Evan," he muttered. The night swallowed his words.

After what felt like an eternity, he glanced at his watch. Eleven minutes. His arms trembled with fatigue, but he couldn't stop. Wouldn't stop. The trail was two miles long. Help was still at least ten minutes away.

He switched to counting aloud to maintain a consistent rhythm as exhaustion set in. "Twenty-seven, twenty-eight, twenty-nine, thirty."

He entered a meditative state, his focus shrunk down to the movement of his tired, burning arms and the corresponding count. He acknowledged his discomfort without judging or becoming attached to it. Acceptance.

When he heard voices echoing in the distance and the thud of running feet, it took a moment for him to return to his surroundings.

"Here!" he shouted toward the beams of light bouncing toward him through the darkness. "We're here!"

He twisted to look over his shoulder, expecting to see first responders, but Tripp and Lucas, came into view, running. When they reached him, Lucas bent over, palms on his knees, sucking down air. Tripp held out a bright red case. An automated external defibrillator.

"Here," he panted. "Aaron sent us to a church just over the bridge to get it while he went to meet the paramedics."

Bodhi continued compressing Evan's chest and blinked up at them. "How did he know Evan would go into cardiac arrest?"

Tripp shrugged. "I don't know. He said to grab it just in case, so we did."

"Aaron just saved a life."

Sometimes a heart attack could disrupt the heart's rhythm and cause sudden cardiac arrest. However Aaron had come by this knowledge, Bodhi was grateful that he had.

Evan's odds of survival with thirty minutes of CPR alone were grim, at best. Bodhi had known all along that saving him would be a long shot. But the addition of the AED changed everything.

"How do we use it?" Tripp asked.

Bodhi gave instructions while he administered chest compressions. "Turn it on. Lucas, while I keep working, attach one pad to his upper right chest and the other on his lower left chest. Below his armpit."

Tripp switched on the machine while Lucas fumbled with the backing on pads. The AED began to issue audio prompts. Lucas connected the pads to the AED. When it was ready to analyze Evan's heart rhythm, Bodhi stepped back and let his arms hang at his sides like lead.

"Clear," he said, following protocol.

They waited while the device worked. Then the mechanical voice announced: "Shock advised. Charging."

Bodhi tore his eyes away from Evan's pale, gray face and met Lucas's gaze. "Be ready to push the button when it flashes."

Lucas swallowed and nodded.

"Stay clear of patient," the AED intoned. "Push the orange button."

The button flashed, and Lucas pressed it.

"Shock delivered."

They waited in tense silence. At the two-minute mark, the machine said, "Perform CPR now."

Bodhi stepped forward, lifted his heavy arms, and resumed the chest compressions.

They repeated the entire clear, analyze, shock,

wait, and chest compression sequence once more before Aaron and two EMTs raced into view.

Bodhi kept compressing Evan's chest, while the professionals dropped their equipment and took over for Lucas and Tripp with precise, efficient movements.

"How long has he been down?" the female EMT asked.

"Almost thirty minutes," Bodhi answered, his voice strained. "Twelve minutes of chest compressions only, until the AED arrived. He had a myocardial infarction. Before I could get him to chew and swallow an aspirin, he collapsed. No pulse, agonal breathing initially, then nothing."

"Aaron says you're a doc?"

"Yes."

"This guy was lucky." Then she commanded, "Stand clear."

Bodhi backed away.

The machine analyzed Evan's rhythm, then delivered a shock that made his body jerk.

The male EMT took over the compressions while his partner prepared an IV and epinephrine.

Bodhi sank to the ground and rested against a tree.

After the third shock, the male EMT announced, "We've got a rhythm."

Bodhi exhaled shakily. Aaron clapped him on the back and handed him a bottle of water.

The EMTs stabilized Evan quickly—oxygen mask, IV fluids, medications—then transferred him to a portable stretcher designed for wilderness evacuation.

"He's got a chance, thanks to you," the female EMT told Bodhi as they prepared to move out.

He shook his head. "It was a group effort. Without Aaron's quick thinking to get an AED and Tripp and Lucas's help, the compressions wouldn't have been enough."

The male EMT gave him a nod. "We called in a 'chopper to airlift him to Pittsburgh from the trailhead."

As the first responders disappeared into the trees, Aaron radioed Sadie to give her the update. She told him they were on their way back and had seen no signs of Rory.

Bodhi leaned his head back and closed his eyes for a moment.

When he opened them, Tripp said, "We never made it to the history center."

Bodhi shook his head. "She's not there."

"How can you know?"

"Evan has Rory's blood on his shoe. He saw her in the cave today. He collapsed before I could confirm it, but I'm pretty sure he's been steering away from wherever he thinks she is."

Aaron exploded. "Does he want her to die?"

"I think," Bodhi said in a weary voice, "he wanted her to stay missing long enough to generate more attention for the plight of the displaced."

"Christ," Lucas muttered.

Tripp had picked up Rory's discarded camera and was scrolling through the images. He paused on a photo of an old house—the only one remaining in a row of demolished structures.

"What's this?" he asked.

Aaron leaned forward. "That's Edward Kovalic's place. It's the last house standing on Company Row."

Bodhi squinted at it. "Can you enlarge it?"

Tripp did.

Bodhi studied the image for a long moment then pulled out his radio. "Diana, come in."

After a moment of static, Diana's voice crackled through. "Go ahead, Bodhi."

"I think I know where Rory is. Call for help. Have them send an ambulance to Company Row."

He pulled himself to his feet and turned to Aaron, "Take me to Kovalic's house."

31

———

The Kovalic House, Company Row

Rory's eyes fluttered open to darkness again. The air was still and stale. Pain radiated through her abdomen in waves, each one more intense than the last.

She tried to orient herself, making out vague shapes in the gloom—a chair, a rough-hewn table, a stone fireplace. Moonlight filtered through dirt-streaked windows, casting weak silver beams across the wooden floor where she lay.

This place felt familiar. A memory flickered through the confusion: an old man on a porch, light striping his weathered face, an excavator reflected in the window behind him.

"Edward Kovalic," she breathed.

She was in the last house standing on Company Row.

How had she gotten here? The last thing she remembered was turning to see Evan in the mouth of the cave. Then pain slicing through her middle as she fell.

More fragmented memories flashed in her mind. Dragging herself through undergrowth to the trail, drawn to this doomed structure—a symbol of resistance, this last man standing against the tide of so-called progress.

Another wave of pain crashed through her, and she curled into herself, gasping. Barbed wire ripped through her intestines, tearing her apart from the inside. Her muscles spasmed and tremors ran.

Seizure incoming.

The tremors intensified, and darkness began to close in from the edges of her vision. Somewhere in the distance, voices called her name. Auditory hallucinations, she thought.

As she slipped out of consciousness, Rory's last coherent thought was that she, like the homes being demolished, would return to dust.

32

———

Bodhi and Aaron sprinted onto the porch of the lonely house standing alone in a sea of rubble.

"Rory!" Aaron shouted.

The front door was unlocked. Bodhi pushed it open. The hinges creaked in loud protest.

"Rory Westin?" he called. His voice echoed in the empty house.

They rushed inside. Their headlamps created wild dancing shadows on the bare walls. And through an open doorway, the light fell on a crumpled figure sprawled on the wood floor.

"Rory!" Aaron rushed forward, but Bodhi caught his arm.

"Careful. Don't touch her," he warned.

Rory lay on her side, her body curled into a fetal position. Her fair skin was tinged blue, and her white-blonde hair was matted with dried blood. As Bodhi's light swept over her, her body convulsed in a violent tremor then went rigid.

"She's seizing."

He dropped to his knees beside her. He tore off his fleece jacket and bundled it under her head to cushion her skull. Then he dug through his pack until he found the apple Will had given him that morning. It felt like a thousand years had passed since then. He used his pocketknife to cut off several tiny pieces.

"What should I do?" Aaron asked, his voice trembling.

"Use your satellite phone to call for an update on the ambulance. Then radio Diana and let her know we found Rory."

Aaron gulped and backed out of the room, headed for the porch to make the calls.

Bodhi gently rolled Rory onto her side to prevent aspiration if she vomited. After a torturously long moment, her seizure subsided and she went limp.

"Rory," Bodhi called softly, touching her shoulder. "Can you hear me?"

Her eyelids fluttered, and a low moan escaped her lips.

"I need you to try to eat something sweet," Bodhi said, holding a piece of apple to her mouth. "It will help."

To his relief, she parted her lips slightly, allowing him to place the fruit on her tongue.

"Chew if you can," he encouraged.

Aaron returned, his face ashen. "Diana's on her way with Julie. The police and an ambulance are en route."

Bodhi nodded, focusing on feeding Rory small bites of apple. Each piece she managed to swallow would help.

After a few minutes, her eyes opened more fully, light dawning in their blue depths.

"My camera …," she murmured.

"I have it. It's safe," he assured her.

Her gaze drifted to the window, where moonlight streamed in. "Should have one more shot. The light …."

"Rest now. Pictures later."

But Rory's expression turned urgent. "No, please. I need it."

Bodhi nodded to Aaron. "Get her camera from my pack."

While Aaron retrieved the camera, Bodhi carefully gathered Rory into his arms, supporting her weight as he lifted her to a seated position.

"What do you want to photograph?" he asked.

Her eyes, clearer now, focused on the window where the moon illuminated the rubble outside—all that remained of Company Row. "Me. The house. The last ones standing."

Aaron handed Bodhi the camera, and he held it out, framing Rory against the moonlit window. Her pale face, the dried blood on her temple, and the determination in her eyes told a story more powerful than anything she could have staged.

Bodhi pressed the shutter just as headlights swept across the window. The sound of vehicles pulling up outside broke the moment.

Police Chief Ron Mercer was the first through the door, followed by a paramedic with a medical bag.

"Diana and Julie called. Ganged up on me and read me the riot act about not taking this seriously," the police chief said in a chastened tone.

The paramedic checked Rory's vital signs while Bodhi explained her condition.

"She has acute intermittent porphyria. She's having an attack, complicated by a head injury."

The medic nodded. "We need to get her down to Pittsburgh. It's the closest place with Level I trauma centers."

"Can I ride with her?" Aaron asked.

The medic nodded. "If it's okay with the patient."

"Yes," she whispered in a weak voice.

Ron jerked his head. "Come on, doc. I'll give you a lift into town and you can fill me it on what in the Sam Hill happened."

PART IV

[T]o see the world around us and the moments that fill our lives as having meaning and beauty that are permanent. This is the art way of seeing[.]

— LEN BERNSTEIN, AMERICAN
PHOTOGRAPHER AND AESTHETIC
REALIST

To see clearly is poetry, prophecy, and religion, all in one.

— JOHN RUSKIN, ENGLISH ART
CRITIC

33

———————

University of Pittsburgh Medical Center
the next day

Rory woke to the soft beeping of monitors and the bleachy smell of stiff hospital sheets. Daylight filtered through the Venetian blinds, casting thin stripes across the institutional beige walls. Her head throbbed dully, but her knife-like abdominal pain had subsided to a manageable ache.

A soft knock at the door drew her attention. The resident who was managing her care stood in the doorway, gripping a wheelchair.

"You have a visitor," Dr. Garcia said. "If you're up for it."

Rory's eyes fell to the chair's occupant. Evan Jeffries, wearing a hospital gown and wristband. His legs covered by a thin, scratchy blanket. He looked old and tired.

"Okay."

The doctor wheeled him into the room and to the

bedside. She engaged the brake on the chair and gave Rory a serious look. "I'll give you two some privacy, but you need rest. You both do. I'll be back in three minutes."

She left, and a heavy silence blanketed the room.

Finally, Evan spoke. "Rory, I—there's no excuse." He clutched the plastic side rail on her bed so tightly that his knuckles turned white. "I found you in that cave, saw you were hurt, and panicked. I ran."

Rory studied him. The righteous activist, the passionate historian who documented the bravery of others, had crumbled in the face of an actual crisis? It seemed impossible.

"Why? No BS, Evan. Really, why?"

He hung his head. "I convinced myself you'd be fine, that you weren't badly hurt. And ... that your disappearance would draw more attention to your work."

She stared at him.

After a beat, he said, "I was right about that, by the way. I don't know if you've been online, but your photographs have gone viral. If I'd known about your condition, I never would have left you. I swear. But all's well that ends well, right?" He raised his eyes and gave her a hopeful look.

She broke eye contact and swallowed hard. Then she pressed the call button. "Professor Jeffries and I are done talking. He's ready to leave."

She leaned back and closed her eyes, keeping them closed when the door opened, Evan was wheeled away, and the door clicked softly closed behind him.

The next time she opened them, Police Chief Ron

Mercer and his ex-wife stood in her open doorway. She blinked.

"I'm surprised to see you two together," she managed.

Diana laughed. "That makes three of us. Can we come in?"

Rory nodded.

Diana crossed the room and squeezed Rory's hand. Then she placed a vase of bright spring flowers on the bedside table. "You worried us."

"I worried me," Rory replied with a laugh.

"The doctor said you're going to be okay."

She nodded and gestured toward the IV line in her left arm. "They gave me intravenous hemin to treat my AIP. I have a mild concussion so they want to keep me overnight. But I'll be fine."

Ron, still in the doorway, shifted his weight from one foot to the other. "Look, I need to know if you want to press charges against Evan Jeffries. Abandoning an injured person, failure to report—"

"No. No charges."

The chief frowned. "He left you to die."

"And he'll have to live with that knowledge." Rory turned toward the flowers and smiled at the cheerful riot of colors. "And the knowledge that I see him for what he truly is."

34

———————

*Allen & Sons Factory, home of the Tri-Town Center
halfway between Clayton Falls and Union Hill,
Four months later*

Diana Mercer stood on the loading dock of the old garment factory, her yellow-tinted glasses bringing into focus the workers and volunteers who carried lumber and tools through the cavernous main entrance. The summer day buzzed with activity.

Julie approached, blueprint in hand, her designer boots somehow immaculate despite the copious construction dust.

"The treatment center will be ready next month," Julie said, pointing to the east wing. "Eight beds to start, with room to expand."

They walked inside together, where the morning light streamed through newly repaired windows. The factory floor had been divided into defined spaces: a community workshop where people could share their expertise in cooking, sewing, carpentry, mechanics, dance, and anything else they could imagine; an art studio with windows that faced the mountains; a large common area with mismatched, comfortable furniture; and the crown jewel, the Bodhi King Addiction Treatment Center, funded with seed money that Rory had raised by auctioning off the photograph she'd had Bodhi take of her at the Kovalic house. Rumor was Tripp had bought it, but nobody knew for sure.

"Not exactly luxury lofts," Diana observed.

Julie smiled ruefully. "Nope. Although those are coming along nicely, too."

Diana laughed. Julie would always be a business woman, but her edges were softer now.

Rory's voice called from the mezzanine above. "Julie! Can you check this lighting?"

They looked up to see Rory adjusting track lighting in what would become the community gallery space. Her exhibition had returned from its three-city tour, and would be permanently housed here—photographs documenting both displacement and resilience along the trail.

As they climbed the metal stairs to join her, Diana remarked, "I never thought I'd see the three of us working together like this."

"Strange bedfellows," Julie agreed.

"Speaking of strange bedfellows," Rory said, gesturing toward the main entrance.

Lydia Hudson stood in the doorway, cardboard boxes stacked in her arms. She wore practical shoes and a determined expression.

"You sure you have room for my canning supplies?" she called up to them.

"Second floor, north corner," Julie responded, surprising Diana with the warmth in her voice. "Your tables are being delivered this afternoon."

The first workshop of the Clayton Falls—Clarksville—Union Hill Community Sustainability Series was a three-parter on creating nutritious meals on a budget. Lydia would teach how to preserve fruits and vegetables by canning and pickling them; Dot would show how to cook affordable plant-based meals to stretch a dollar; and her nephew, Will, and his daughter, Jessie, home from college for the summer, were going to teach an easy system of container gardening, rain barrel irrigation, and composting.

Camden and Joey hurried to help Lydia with her boxes. Joey, newly clean, had been hired as a peer counselor for the addiction center. His younger friend Camden was enrolled in Julie's entrepreneurship program, his nervous energy channeled into planning a bike repair business to serve trail users.

The three women adjusted the lighting and then leaned on the railing to look down at the space they were transforming together—not into something new and shiny that erased what came before, but into something that honored the building's history while serving the present community. A third space, as Rory had called it in her proposal. Not luxury, not abandonment, but something vital in between.

"Did you hear about Aaron and Sadie?" Julie asked.

Diana's eyes widened. "No, what? Please tell me he didn't propose."

Julie laughed, "No. Much better. He got the promotion. Sadie said after he came through in the emergency for Evan and Rory, he had so much more confidence that all his poor performance issues evaporated. She recommended him to replace her as store manager, and he aced the interview."

Rory beamed. "Does that mean she's starting her bike tours soon?"

"It does. She signed her lease this morning. She'll be the first official tenant at the new business incubator." Julie gave Rory a sidelong glance. "The new, smaller business incubator that leaves room for a playground and ball fields at the Patch."

Rory snorted. "You know it'll attract families."

"I do. That's why I agreed to it. You didn't think it was all because of your dazzling smile, did you?"

Their laughter faded when Evan Jeffries appeared on the floor below, carrying a large box.

Diana pointed her chin at him. "How's he doing?"

Rory blew out a breath. "He resigned as director of the history center and from the university. He says he needs a fresh start. He bought a camper and he and his cat are going to travel around the country. He might write a book. I don't know if I'm supposed to feel bad or—?"

"Nope." Diana told her. "You're not. What's in the boxes?"

Rory shrugged. "No idea."

Julie supplied the answer. "When he was downsizing to sell his cottage, he came across some personal books and photos he'd collected over the years about the founding of the three towns. The history center didn't want them, so he offered to donate them to us."

As if he sensed them talking about him, as soon as Camden took the box from his arms, he looked up. Rory lifted a hand and waved. He beamed as he waved back. Then he ducked his head and hurried back outside.

35

GAP Mile 0, Cumberland, Maryland
one month later

The Great Allegheny Passage terminated in a small park in Cumberland, Maryland, where it connected with the C&O Canal Towpath. A simple stone marker indicated the trail's official endpoint, a quiet celebration of the journey completed.

Bodhi stood in front of the marker, his pack light on his shoulders after days of hiking. He'd returned to the trail in late summer, drawn back to restart and complete the journey that had been interrupted. Along the way, he'd stopped to revisit the communities and people who had become unexpectedly important to him.

And now, he'd reached the end of the path. He'd finally completed the full trail, from Pittsburgh to

Cumberland, moving at his own pace, observing the changing landscape with clear eyes.

Summer was in full bloom in the valley. Wild roses, fragrant and delicate, bordered the park. In the wildflower meadows, purple sage, cornflower, and bee balm rose from the grass, waving in the breeze as fat bees and elegant butterflies danced through the fields.

Bodhi settled on a bench overlooking the Upper Potomac. Sunlight sparkled on the river's surface, glinting silver. He removed his kraft journal from his pack and opened it to a fresh page to record his reflections on the final day of his journey.

He bent his head and began to write in his small, neat printing:

> A journey that began as a solitary quest for clarity, a chance to walk alone with my thoughts, became something far more complex and valuable—a lesson in the power of collective vision, in the importance of seeing beyond oneself.

He wrote faster, filling the page and then another.

When a shadow fell over his journal, he looked up.

A tall, slender figure with distinctive white-blonde hair stood over him, a camera hanging around her neck.

"I heard a rumor you'd be here," Rory said.

He closed the journal and stood. "And here I am."

"Diana said you planned to take the bus back to Pittsburgh tomorrow."

He nodded. "That's right."

"Well, we're having a community potluck at the Tri-Town Center tonight. There'll be lots of vegan options, and we thought you might like to join us. Julie's waiting in the parking area, with the AC running in her car. Can't let her makeup melt." She laughed. "And Aaron can give you a lift back to Pittsburgh after dinner. He's got a late flight out to OAC's corporate headquarters for some training seminar. There are a lot of people who'd love to see you."

A slow smile spread across his face. "I'd like that, too."

He was part of many communities—his sangha, his circle of friends back home, and the people he encountered in his travels. Every community offered something different. Tonight, in addition to friendship, this one just might offer Dot's delicious chickpea salad followed by a slice of Will's vegan carrot cake.

He returned his journal to the bag and followed Rory to the parking lot. They stopped halfway there so she could squat in the meadow to take a picture of an iridescent blue dragonfly that glittered in the sunlight like a suspended jewel.

AUTHOR'S NOTE

This is the third Bodhi King book in a row that
touches on ideas of community and taking care of one
another. Following on the heels of *Chosen Path* and
Forgotten Path, Bodhi once again helps a town heal
from a trauma and grow stronger in the aftermath.

The Great Allegheny Passage is a real 150-mile trail
that runs from Pittsburgh, Pennsylvania, to Cumberland, Maryland. The towns of Clayton Falls,
Clarksville, and Union Hill are fictional—although
the challenges they face are all too real.

The other theme running through this book is vision
and perception—how we see others and ourselves
and how that colors our interactions. Rory's actions
and her disappearance are judged by the way people
respond to her physical beauty. Diana's vision condition impacts both how she is seen and how she sees.

Bodhi, as always, sees things as they truly are. In his

latest adventure, he also realizes, as the English poly-
math John Ruskin put it, way back in 1872, "You do not
see *with* the lens of the eye. You see *through* that, and
by means of that, but you see with the soul of the
eye."[1]

I hope your eyes, and your soul, and your heart show
you the good and the beautiful in this flawed and
scarred world.

Melissa
March 2025

---

1.   John Ruskin, Lecture VI, *The Relation to Art of the Science of Light*,
February, 24 1872.

THANK YOU!

Thank you for reading *Clear Path!*

You can find an up-to-date list of *all* my books at melissafmiller.com.

ABOUT THE AUTHOR

USA Today bestselling author Melissa F. Miller majored in English literature with concentrations in creative writing poetry and medieval literature. Upon graduating from college, she was stunned to learn that there's not a robust job market for such a degree. After working as an editor for several years, she returned to school to earn a law degree.

After fifteen years, including a stint as a clerk for a federal judge, nearly a decade as an attorney at major international law firms, and several years running a two-person law firm with her lawyer-husband, she traded the practice of law for the art of telling stories.

Now, powered by coffee, she writes full time from the Pennsylvania home she shares with her family and their cat and dog. (The cat's in charge.)